Imagine Me and You

Lynn Camden

Contents

For all my kindred spirits: the writers and readers of romance. It is a privilege to be one of you, to learn from you, and to squeal and swoon over our beloved books together. I hope I've added a worthy love story to the mix.

And for EJ, always.

Content Notes

Please be aware that this book includes mentions of hoarding, mentions of alcoholism and abuse (historic, off page), and descriptive sex scenes.

"Love is friendship set on fire." — Jeremy Taylor

ONE

Simone

"**A**bsolutely not."

"Please, James. Please?" Simone shifted the phone to a more secure position against her shoulder and grabbed the bag of cat food, nearly tripping over the yowling cats twining around her ankles. All cats wished death on the ones who fed them. It was a simple rule of the universe.

Erica, the co-director of their animal shelter, peered in from the other side of the glass. She'd been badgering Simone about this call all damn week. If she'd had a free hand, she would have shooed Erica away. The fewer witnesses, the better, for what was sure to be an epic grovel.

"Are you even paying attention? You called *me*, remember?" His voice rose in a familiar pattern of stress that had her wincing. This tone was never a good sign. "I still remember the last time I followed you on one of your harebrained schemes. You were eighteen and your parents still grounded you for a month! *Grounded,* at that age! And I never got the smell of cat pee out of my car mats."

"That was a long time ago, J," she said gently. She could picture his expression over the phone. His fingers would be pinching the bridge of his nose, lifting his glasses, trying to relieve the stress of her request. "As I recall, that car was a junker with two doors that didn't open, windows that stuck, and it didn't smell great even when you first bought it. We've both moved on to better cars and better things. My schemes for rescuing cats usually work these days." The cats gazed intently at her, their cries intensifying by the second. She couldn't help but laugh. Better get this show on the road.

"Insulting the old Saturn isn't going to win you any points."

"Okay, okay, I get it. But this is not about me. Gran said I needed to come with a date, that it was absolutely necessary." She trailed off. That was bothering her, too. Gran was usually breezy and vague, but she'd been almost sharp during that call, her anxiety humming over the line. Gran had even suggested paying James in company stock. Only a strong sense of granddaughterly loyalty kept her from confessing her doubts to James right now.

"Sense skips a generation in your family."

Ouch.

Bending down, she filled the cat bowls around her, then checked the water level in the fountains. Cats came running from all the perches around the room and settled to eat. A few loners who didn't get along with the others were kept in separate areas. They'd get fed before she closed up for the night. Erica was taking care of the birds at the moment, along with the one rabbit they had taken in.

James waited silently on the other end of the line as she slid out of the cat room, automatically blocking a would-be escape artist with her toe. He had to be fuming. She should have called after she'd rehearsed this and prepared a compelling argument. But she'd been slammed all week, and the event was looming. She had a promise to keep.

"Come on...it's one weekend. What can I do to convince you?" She cast around for something, anything, to entice him. Erica stood at the front desk, running through her closing checklist. She gave Simone a sympathetic shrug and a headshake that sent her black hair swinging. She was no help at all. The concrete walls of Helping Paws offered no inspiration, either.

Which buttons could she press to get this robot, who sounded like her friend, to live a little? "I...can detail your car! Every week for a month. Six months!"

"You suck at car washes. You'd have to be detailed to detail, Simone."

Ouch again. Point two to James.

"I'm detailed. When it's interesting enough. When it counts."

"Right. But none of that applies to my Civic. Pass."

Well, at least she had his attention. He was settling into negotiator mode, which meant she was most of the way there. She pictured one of his long, lean hands sweeping through his short-cropped copper curls as he considered, his pale, freckled face pinched and stern. Idly, she wondered if he was still in work clothes, or in one of those loose tees that draped so perfectly off his clothes-hanger shoulders. He'd always ignored her hints that he had a great frame for modeling. He cared about clothes like he cared about his car: that they were clean, functional, comfortable, and appropriate for the occasion. Blending in was his priority. Not a goal she'd ever been able to relate to, fashion-wise.

"I'll cook for you. For a month. And make you a pie." She wasn't much of a precision baker, but a good pie was made by feel, and she'd learned the knack young.

The silence stretched and her grin stretched with it. She nearly had him; she could almost feel him wavering through the distance separating them.

"Three months. And I want pie once a week." He hesitated. "Take it or leave it."

Of course he'd be capable of packing all that food away every week. Suddenly, she had doubts. Cooking for him would quadruple her grocery bill. Could she really afford that, just to help Gran out of a bind?

Though really, it was Simone who was in a bind now, thanks to whatever Gran had started. Maybe she'd foot Simone's impending grocery bill in exchange for her silence. Gran's relationship with Simone's mother had always been a little strained, and Gran wouldn't want to further alienate her daughter-in-law, if Simone reported these latest antics. Maybe that was manipulative, but it was the kind of calculus that was necessary in her family.

The pause had stretched too long. If she let him think about it even one more minute, he'd back out. "Done."

He groaned on the other end of the line. She smiled in triumph. There was no doubt in her mind she'd sealed the deal just in time.

"When do we do this?" he asked, full of resignation.

"Next weekend." Another groan. This one held the sweet note of defeat. She knew his groans well; she had caused practically all of them. She could parse their distinct sounds like a vintner sipping wine for tasting notes. Exasperation and frustration were common, of course, but he had happy ones too. His contented sigh after an epic meal, or his noise of mock-frustration when he tried to explain the strategy for one of his beloved board games. It didn't matter how many times they played; strategy just slid off her brain.

Another smile curved her lips. The best of his groans was the one he made when she won one of those maddening games by pure luck, playing at random, yet suddenly ending up with everything. That sound was the most satisfying: it was mystified, a little awed, and a lot annoyed.

"What do I need to pack?" His question called her back to the present.

"It's just two nights. So enough for the weekend. Casual stuff for outdoor events, and then something more formal for the ball."

"How formal? Black tie? White tie? Cocktail? Semi-formal?" He should have been an interrogator instead of an accountant.

"Are all those different things for menswear?"

"Yes, of course they are."

"Well excuse me, Mr. High Society. I had no idea you were so well versed."

"Simone, your family owns half of the fancy hotels around. Who's the high society one here?"

She waved her hand dismissively, even though he couldn't see it. "It's not my family, it's Gran's family. Or my aunt's family, anyway. And, as my mother says, they're 'nouveau riche et très gauche.' You know that."

"Still counts. You still attend balls and shit. Here's the thing, Simone. You might feel like you can do whatever the hell you want. But some of us actually have to pay attention to how we come across. We don't all have an eccentric grandmother to make excuses for us."

There was no catching the tiny sigh before it escaped. He knew her so well, and yet there were some things he either couldn't or wouldn't understand about her family.

"Gran loves you, James. You know she'd make any excuse you needed."

"That's not the point, Simone. The point is that if you expect to rope me into this, I need a detailed dress code for every single event."

That tone. It clearly indicated the bridge pinching was back. She was suddenly tempted to take the call to video to catch him with his hand tucked under his glasses. She smiled just picturing it. Somehow, seeing it would make this whole call better.

"Fine. My dad knows menswear—I could ask him. Oh, wait. They'll be away, and frankly, the less they know the better. I don't need any more drama. I'll have to ask Sam.

She'll know." Her cousin was always very organized. She'd have an itinerary sent over within minutes, or her assistant would.

"Fine yourself. And I expect my first meal tomorrow."

So snippy. "Thanks, James! You're the best!" She put extra pep into it, just to irk him, and slipped the phone into her pocket to finish her rounds. Somehow, when Gran got in one of her scrapes, Simone was the one who ended up doing all the work to fix it. Now she was going to have to make a grocery list, a meal plan, and put together a detailed dress code. And what did Gran have to do? Oh, that's right, nothing. She'd swan in and sparkle, mischief gleaming in her eyes. And inevitably, Simone would find herself forgiving Gran for all the extra hours that had gone into pulling off another ridiculous farce.

TWO

James

The car ride with Simone had been a slice of bliss. The sun high overhead, the road unfurling in gentle curves. Towering trees bracketed their path, making him feel small and isolated from everyone else in the world, except for his copilot. She'd smile at him, commenting over the music, bringing up old memories and past road trips, then update him on which rescue pup was currently making off with her heart. From the depths of one of her three bags, she'd fish out snacks, then unearth his favorite flavor of fizzy water, triumphantly laughing at his surprise. The drinks had been miraculously cool, crisp and refreshing, just like her. He could have kept driving forever.

All perfect moments must eventually end. No matter how long they lasted.

Only after parking, as he sat clenching the car keys, did he realize how tense he was. His stomach's churning was not just because he'd had too many pistachios, and his headache was not solely from the sun's glare. He had no idea how this weekend would go, but he didn't think there'd be anything good in it. At least he could claim introvert time, hiding in his room as much as possible. Simone would understand. She would make excuses for him.

Shit. She was already at the trunk, wrangling too many bags. He hopped out to help, shaking away the tension in his hands and rolling his shoulders to release them.

"Your jaw is going to get stuck like that," she teased, heaving at her enormous suitcase with a cute grunt.

He grabbed its other handle, helping her pull it from the trunk. "Chicks dig a clenched jaw. It's all masculine and shit."

"Sure. Keep telling yourself that." She chuckled, rolling her suitcase the short distance to the boardwalk, leaving him staring at the swish of her dress and the bounce of her long brown hair.

He lifted his own bag, jogged a few steps to catch up, then tugged gently at one of her shoulder bag's straps until she let him carry it. He eyed her big rolling suitcase. Should he offer to take that too? No, she'd shoot him down and tell him her arms were working just fine.

They were nearly at the dock and had somehow managed to not discuss a single important thing on the entire drive. What had he been thinking?

"Simone, wait." He had to step partly into her path to stop her from plowing ahead. "We're supposed to be dating? Will we have to do anything couple-ish?"

Sliding her big cat-eye sunglasses down her nose, she inspected him. "I mean, I don't think we'll have to make out or anything. PDA makes people uncomfortable anyway." She smiled brightly, only deepening his suspicions. "I'm sure some handholding will be fine. You can suffer through occasionally putting your arm around me. That'll be the worst of it."

There was nothing to say to that, really. He stepped out of her way with a nod and they kept walking toward the big dock. The boat would take them to the resort on the other side of Bear Lake.

Simone nudged him with her elbow. "Relax, J. It'll be fine. Gran will meet us there and give us our room keys. You can interrogate her to your heart's content."

He snorted. "Mrs. Larson better have a good reason for all this."

"She was a little vague on the details. She might have been a few martinis deep when I tried to get an explanation."

They joined the small gathering crowd, whose mood was decidedly festive for just past noon.

"Speaking of martinis, are we the only ones who didn't have a liquid lunch?" He whispered the words, but he needn't have bothered lowering his voice. Everyone waiting to board seemed to have had their midday cocktails with a side of gin. If they weren't careful, someone was going to fall into the water.

He tugged Simone away from the loud, tipsy crowd, leaving their larger bags with the rest of the luggage waiting to be loaded.

The minutes stretched on in the beating sun. He wished he were back in an air-conditioned car, sipping a drink his fake girlfriend had packed for him for real. Sighing, he rubbed at his chest.

Simone, meanwhile, was twirling in place to keep herself entertained, letting her sundress flare. The sunflower print haloed around her, then hugged her legs, lifting enough to show bright yellow bike shorts beneath her dress. She usually cited "chub rub" as the reason she wore shorts with her dresses, but he'd known her long enough to suspect it had to be partly so that if she decided to roll down a hill or try to climb a tree, she'd still be covered. Simone never had been able to sit still.

Her dress had complicated straps that held her breasts in a gravity-defying way, looping around her neck and crisscrossing her upper back. No bra straps. She looked like an even lusher 50s pinup. Not that he was looking at her that way. He was simply observant.

He remembered when they were both eleven, she'd solemnly informed him how much she'd hated shopping for her first bra and that boobs were the worst. He'd swallowed his embarrassment and nodded, equally grave, and avoided looking at the area in question. During the sixteen intervening years, he'd mastered the art of not looking directly at her cleavage. But it was always there.

One of the drunken idiots stumbled too close, nearly knocking Simone over. Grabbing her arm, James pulled her out of the man's path, turning a shoulder to shield her.

"'Scuse me," the man slurred. It was an alcohol-soaked mishap, judging by the hue of his veiny red cheeks. Through squinted eyes, he leered disgustingly at Simone before shuffling down the wide dock. James' heart pounded in his chest, his hands still clutching Simone's waist.

He glared after the man, his jaw tight.

"It's okay, J. I'm fine."

Her voice called him back and he looked down into her worried eyes. She knew his history. She always checked on him.

He abruptly realized she was plastered against him. Her back curved against his front, her soft parts molding to him in perfect yet disturbing ways. She didn't seem to notice. Her head was tipped back to look at him, giving him a top view of her pale cleavage, impossible to avoid seeing from this angle. His eyes flicked back to her face.

Wait, that was worse. Full, red lips parted in a half smile, light brown eyes shining with reassurance, cute little nose scrunched, waiting for him to respond. She was all delight and temptation. All he had was his usual defense—but whatever that was didn't come to mind. Well, he may have been defenseless against her, but she didn't have to know it.

"Hey, Simone? Why don't we turn around and go home?" His voice had turned wheedling, his arms still locked around her. "We could pick up a London Fog for you, some donuts, and go play Ticket to Ride. You can stay in my spare bedroom—you have your stuff packed, anyway. I'll make you pancakes. You can pick our Saturday movie marathon. Even if it's *Scream* one through one hundred, I won't complain."

He was describing their perfect weekend. And although her eyes sparkled and her smile widened, puffing her round cheeks into biteable apples, he knew she wasn't going to budge.

"James. I promised Gran we would come. And Uncle Dick practically ordered me to be here. This is important to the family. They want this opening to go well. Oh look, the boat is boarding—it's time to go!"

She slipped out of his grip like water, picking up her shoulder bags from where they sat at her feet. She was halfway down the dock before he reacted, hastily lifting his share of the luggage and following. He was always trailing in her wake.

THREE
Simone

Gran was on the dock waiting for them, waving enthusiastically. Short, pale, plump, silver-haired, and dressed in head-to-toe turquoise, she stood out among the muted colors of the crowd. Today, her Capri pants matched her tank top and the beaded shawl draped over her upper arms. It wouldn't matter if had been hotter than the desert: Gran would cover that "problem area."

Simone waved back, her own arms bared proudly, grinning to herself as she felt them jiggle. After years of going to the mall with friends just to buy jewelry and accessories at straight-size-only stores, she was free. Online shopping meant she could look like the Pink Lady of her dreams, and the world could pry her halter dresses from her cold, dead hands.

"James! You're looking as handsome as ever." Gran was laying it on thick, holding both arms out toward him, the fringe of her shawl swaying. James dutifully folded himself in half to have his cheek kissed, coming away with a smear of bright pink lipstick on one angular cheekbone.

Simone suppressed the urge to reach up and rub it away, giving Gran a brief hug instead. While Gran chattered at both of them, she smiled up at James, wordlessly motioning to his cheek.

Lately, James had a wall around him that didn't invite touching. It had happened so gradually, she couldn't pinpoint when its foundations had been laid. They'd stopped hugging sometime in high school. After grad, he'd started occasionally sitting on the other side of the couch during movie nights and friend hangs. In college, the gaps in seeing each other had stretched longer: months, then half a year. Their texts, once so easy, had become stilted at best. She'd assumed she'd done something wrong. It must have been her. James always had his reasons.

She shook it off. "What's Misty up to this weekend?" Gran's rescue pup was the light of her life.

"I didn't think she'd like the lake, poor thing." She turned to James flirtatiously. "Misty is deathly afraid of water, the darling. Even rain puddles give her the vapors!" She laughed girlishly and looked back at Simone, not seeming to see James' visibly patient expression. "Erica agreed to take her. She gets along so well with their dogs."

"Gran. When did you rope her into this? You should have just hired someone. Erica has another debut this weekend." A whole cadre of Erica's many Filipina cousins would turn eighteen this year. Every other Monday, Erica limped into their office, looking happily exhausted and complaining about dancing too hard. Simone would joke she should slow down before she needed a hip replacement. There was no way she had time to take care of a fussy, spoiled dog this weekend.

"Darling, she said it was no problem when I swung by this morning. Her eldest will do all the walks. She could use a little extra spending money. Such a sweet child."

Chesa was sweet and fairly responsible at twelve. And if Simone couldn't say no to Gran, she could hardly fault Erica for having the same problem.

James snorted and caught her eye as though he knew exactly what she was thinking. She dropped the subject and let Gran chivvy them off the dock, the rolling wheels of her suitcase clunking over each brand-new board.

James was back in her life, and maybe they didn't quite have what they had when they were younger, but they still had their game nights and movie marathons. And if she missed all those quiet midnights when he would open up to her about his dreams, hopes, and plans, she was grateful to witness him building the life he'd always wanted. He didn't have to share how his dreams were changing. He didn't have to share anything with her.

Everything in the resort was sparklingly new and opulently proportioned. Her relatives were definitely of the more-is-more philosophy, and they'd carried that over to the resort design. A giant hotel lodge was set into the rock, with individual cabins dispersed through the grounds. Simone's stakeholder portfolio boasted of a swimming pool, a hot tub, a beach on the lake with trucked-in sand, and an enormous golf course.

Simone sighed.

James caught her wavelength, the years and distance between them disappearing like magic. "Hey, I wonder how much pristine spruce fell to make way for this faux-log cabin monstrosity?" He muttered it once Gran was safely a few steps ahead. What he didn't understand about her grandmother was that even if she'd heard, she wouldn't have cared.

"I'll have your things sent up for you," Gran called over her shoulder. "We have an appointment on the golf course and can't be late!" She hurried them along the winding stone path to the grand front entrance.

"We'll want to change and freshen up, Gran. James did all the driving and needs a break before diving into whatever you have planned." Her tone was mild, but she needn't have moderated it, as Gran wasn't much for subtlety. Simone would have practically had to yell before she'd even get through to Gran, never mind offend her.

But, as thoughtless as Gran could be, she was the only one consistently on Simone's side. Without her, funding the animal shelter would have been impossible. That kind of loyalty wasn't something she took lightly. Not even James always stood by her. Not that he had to say anything. That particular huff of irritation was enough to let her know how he felt.

"Oh, nonsense. You two young things look fresh as daisies. There's a powder room in the lobby you can use before we go to the green."

James cut in. "Mrs. Larson, I read that there's a dress code for the golf course. Simone and I will have to change."

She trilled another laugh. "Oh, I'm sure they'll make an exception for me."

She really was trying to hustle them. What was so important that they had to go straight to the course?

"Gran, we'll take our room keys now and meet you in half an hour. Surely thirty minutes won't make a difference." Simone dredged up a sunny smile. Honey worked better than vinegar with Gran.

"Oh, well then. I already have your room key. Everything is taken care of, and your bags should be waiting for you. I'll meet you on the course. Don't be late, now!" She bustled off as quickly as her short legs could move, fringed shawl swaying behind her.

James caught Simone's eye, looking confused. "Did she seem even more odd than usual?" His expression became more serious. "You know, bladder infections can affect elderly people. Sometimes it can even make them seem like they've got dementia. Maybe you should check to make sure she's okay."

Simone rolled her eyes. "She'd hardly be racing around the resort with a UTI. I wouldn't exactly call her elderly, either." Only James could have said that with a straight face about a woman who could probably run them both into the ground. She held up the envelope with the key cards, which James took and pried open. "Let's find our rooms. How did you know about the golf course dress code?"

"I checked the website, of course. Simone, I think I should tell you that while I was researching..." He stopped midsentence, glancing into the envelope with narrowed eyes. "Simone."

She ignored the warm feeling she always got from hearing her name in his deep voice and focused on the suspicion in his eyes and his lengthy pause to inhale.

"Is that one room key?" His voice was rising. Never a good sign.

She looked at the evidence. She'd assumed that more than one key was inside. Or that what looked like one key was, instead, two stuck together. But no, it was decidedly one key for one room. Room 305. Worse, both their names were written on the outside of the envelope.

"I think there's been a mistake," she said, for the fifth time. Simone willed herself to patience. This was the third person they'd spoken to at the reception desk. Each had taken some time to tap away at the keyboard, frowning, before calling in a more senior person. It seemed this brand-new resort was still working out the kinks in its reservation system. James was impatiently drumming his fingers on the marble counter. The tempo of his fingers increased, signaling he was close to a breaking point. The line behind them was growing too: people had started to shuffle and raise their voices as the wait dragged on. She had to solve this fast, before someone erupted.

She pulled out her credit card. It was a last resort—she rolled her eyes at her unintentional pun—because there was no way she could afford these room rates if they weren't comped. But anything was better than standing with a powder keg beside her and frustrated guests behind her.

"That's fine. We can keep the reservation and I'll add another room to this card. Can you put that through now, please?" Her tone was pleasant but authoritative, the sort of voice she used when she was dealing with a group of volunteers.

"I'm sorry, Ms. Larson, there are no more rooms available. The hotel is fully booked this weekend." The manager with the sharp blonde bob and even sharper jawline, looked them over appraisingly. "There is a note on your file. Mr. Montgomery congratulates you on your engagement. He's ordered champagne on arrival and comped your room service." Her eyes narrowed in what seemed like suspicion, but she carried on. "If you'll follow Gerry here, he will show you to your room. If you're considering our facilities for your wedding and would like to speak to our event planner, we would be delighted to arrange it while you're here."

The manager gave them another piercing look before apparently dismissing them. With the beginnings of a smile on her face, she lifted her chin toward the next couple, obviously moving the line along.

Simone blinked, still uselessly holding her credit card over the counter. James had gone stiff beside her, his tapping fingers stilled at last. She peeked up at him sideways. He eyed her right back, unreadable.

"Let's go," he said, suddenly decisive. "We'll talk once we're in the room."

She didn't like the sound of that. But she followed him and Gerry, weaving through the crowded lobby, up the gold and oak elevators, right into their room, where Gerry made an awkward show of turning on lights, flinging open curtains, and uncorking their champagne with a flourish.

James hustled him out with a tip as soon as he could, thanking him with obvious effort, then gently closing the door behind him. He turned to her with a hand already tugging at his short curls. He was a study in contrasts: angry but still beautiful. His face had gone blotchy and pale, but the copper highlights in his light brown hair were more prominent in the diffuse light streaming in from the windows and his freckles stood out even more strongly

than usual. She winced, squared her shoulders, and prepared for the explosion. Somehow this was all her fault.

"What the FUCK."

FOUR

James

He shouldn't yell. He hated yelling, hated the reminder that he had a temper. He always tried his hardest to tamp it down, and loathed himself every time he failed.

None of this was her fault.

He paced up and down the hotel room with his hand on his pounding forehead. Well, maybe some of it was a little bit her fault. He couldn't quite bring himself to look at Simone. Why did she have to go along with whatever scheme her grandmother cooked up? The backbone that she showed him often enough was nowhere to be found when Frances was on a roll.

This whole place made him feel sick. The golf course on land that had never seen grass like this before, the trucked-in dirt to cover Canadian Shield rock, the imported sand to create a beach. It was a disgrace. And now he had to be here for the whole weekend, trying to find the balance between not disappointing her and being true to himself.

He had to lie. For her, he would do it, but he hated the idea. It was enough stress for a month of tension headaches.

Simone was nibbling on her cherry-red bottom lip, twisting her fingers, clearly unsure what to say. He hated that they were at odds, but couldn't think of a single thing to make it right.

"You're just going to go along with this, aren't you." It came out flat, his anger cooling into something like resentment. "Frances makes up some ridiculous scheme, and you just fall in line."

"Gran said it was important. I'm sure she wouldn't ask if it wasn't necessary." She lifted her shoulders helplessly. "This is what I do. I'm expected to contribute to the family business when I'm called upon."

"Contribution means lying about an engagement? In what world does that make sense?" He dug his thumb into his right temple, then lifted his glasses to rub at his eyes. They were achy and grainy from the glaring sun on the drive up.

Simone shrugged again, and the dismissal of it lanced another ache into his chest.

"Well, I guess we should change for golf. If we go, we can talk to Gran about getting another room. Or I could go stay in hers."

"No. We're not going to golf. You can call her and tell her that we're not going through with this plan. Pretending to date was one thing. Pretending to be engaged..." His eyes fell on her hands, still twisting nervously. "You don't even have a ring!"

He tamped down his bubbling anger, shutting his mouth tightly. No matter what, he would not yell again. His glasses rose for a second time as he once again pinched the bridge of his nose, willing himself to think. Calmly.

"We're tired from the drive and it's getting late. What we're going to do is order room service and then sort out this room situation. The least your family can do is feed us. And once we figure out the room, I'm going to lie on top of those ten ridiculous pillows on the bed and see what channels they have on satellite and try to forget that I'm here at all." He could deal with almost anything, as long as there was a plan to give order to chaos. He could almost feel his stress level dropping, just from making one.

There was no reason for her to look hurt. She turned away without responding and muscled her bulging suitcase onto the luggage rack.

"That's fine, James. I understand. I shouldn't have asked you to do this. I'll change and go down to the golf course, meet Gran there, and see what I can sort out. You can have dinner and relax—I'll be out of your way. I'll come back for my things once I have a room."

She bent over to rummage through her luggage, her dress hiking slowly up her hips, exposing the dimpled backs of her knees. As she ransacked her packed clothing, her dress slipped up and down, flashing glimpses of thick thighs and those semi-sheer sunshine yellow shorts.

He looked away. There was no need to be a creep. There had to be something to relieve his suddenly parched mouth, other than champagne, of course. He paused by the bottle to pour Simone a flute, setting it beside her on the desk. Even if they weren't truly celebrating, she could enjoy a glass.

There was fancy sparkling water in the mini-fridge. It probably cost a ridiculous amount, but there was not a chance he'd pay for it. Simone's uncle Dick owned the place and could damn well afford to cover the water. Hell, he could probably afford a whole bottling company. He unscrewed the cap, poured it into the second flute, waited a few impatient seconds for the fizz to subside, then tossed it back, without a care for the carbonation. Yes, of course he nearly choked. And wheezed. And gasped for air. Fizzy water 1, James 0.

She turned to him at the sound of his reaction, the concern on her face melting into amusement once she saw what had happened. "Did you just try to shoot that?"

Coughing was the only response he could offer, the bubbles still burning his nose, but he pointed at the champagne he'd poured her and topped his drink up again. It hadn't done much for his throat, but it kept his hands busy.

She picked her glass up with a bright smile of thanks. It didn't take much for her to bounce back to sunny. Alarmingly, he noticed her other hand was holding a garment that was very black and very lacy. He looked away before he could analyze it too closely, tipping his second glass to his mouth at a less aggressive angle. She took a small sip, then kept sorting through her clothes. It looked like she'd brought enough for a week, even without the garment bag casually slung over the back of the chair.

"What does one wear on a golf course, anyway?" She'd come up for air holding something that looked satiny and sleek...and like it didn't contain a lot of fabric, whatever it was. Before he could analyze it further, she stuffed it back into the other side of the suitcase. He was going to go out of his mind if he kept speculating on her lacy, satiny clothes.

"I can't believe you've never golfed. Isn't that what your crowd does?"

She spared him a cutting glance of disdain. "*My crowd* is usually covered in cat scratches and dog kisses on the weekend. The dress code is old jeans and even older t-shirts. I have always managed to avoid golf. Until now."

He spread his hands placatingly. "Did you pack runners? You won't be allowed to wear sandals on the course. And the website said we'd need collared shirts and khakis. I brought a polo and shorts just in case." The likelihood that she owned a collared shirt at all seemed slim. He should have texted her about it, but he hadn't thought they'd be golfing. That wasn't something they did.

This time, when she turned around, she was holding a bra. Why was she taking out all her underwear? The cups were...generous, and the bright pink lace was see-through. He noticed he was tensing his stomach, holding his breath, waiting to see what new marvel he could add to his catalog of her lacy things. Like he was fifteen again. He rolled his eyes at himself and walked to the window to look out on the grounds in the afternoon sun. He was being ridiculous. His Simone-related thoughts usually weren't this bad. The new setting was throwing him off.

Still staring out the window, he kept talking to distract himself. "I can't believe they didn't cover golf attire in your finishing school."

The initial frustration had died down, but he was still on edge. Everything about her was getting under his skin today, in all the worst ways. The feeling that they were going in circles with every conflict, the way the satiny ribbon wrapped around her ponytail was dull compared to the shine of her walnut hair. Getting a meal and watching a movie together was one of his favorite ways to spend an evening. But maybe they could still turn this whole disaster bus around. Maybe if he stalled her long enough, she would miss whatever her grandmother was scheming. Maybe she'd come back and join him. Getting a meal and watching a movie together was one of his favorite ways to spend an evening. He mentally updated their movie-viewing location to the couch instead of the bed. Neutral territory was better.

"If it came up, I don't remember. And it was etiquette classes, not finishing school." Her tone was mild, not rising to his bait. "Runners, I have. I don't have a shirt with a collar. I'll just wear my workout gear and hope it's okay." She resurfaced again from the depths of her suitcase, holding up a bright, strappy spandex number. "Maybe I'll add my tennis skirt to this."

"Why on earth did you pack a tennis skirt?"

"I thought they might have a tennis court!"

"Your family owns this hotel. Hell, you own shares. And you've never once looked on their website or informed yourself about their facilities?"

She waved a hand. "There was a stakeholder binder I flipped through once, but I have my own business to run. What these people do with their hotel isn't my problem. I just show up when they make me and forget about the rest."

"That's really irresponsible—" She cut him off with another wave, this one slashing across her chest, and stalked off to the bathroom.

He sighed. He supposed they'd had a version of this argument before. There was no point in getting into it again.

The last few sips of his sparkling water were warm from his sweaty fist, but he drained the glass and helped himself to more with a deepening sense of resignation. There was no sense in fighting any of it: Simone, or the Montgomery side of the family. They were a force, bulldozing all before them. No one wanted to hear what he had to say. The question was how long he could hold his tongue and still be able to face himself in the mirror.

Simone intruded on his grim line of thinking, emerging in a blinding neon-green top with matching shorts underneath a flirty, pleated white skirt. She looked like a green-apple-flavored candy. Tiny straps crossed intricately over her cleavage, which was molded into new heights. She made him dizzy sometimes.

"I don't think they're going to let you on the course with all that skin showing," he said, with an attempt at wryness. She looked down at herself as though wondering what he was talking about. As if they hadn't just had a conversation about a course dress code.

"Oh, it's fine. I'm sure it will be fine."

"Do you have something with sleeves? Should I loan you my polo shirt?"

"Are you nuts? It's scorching out. Everything I brought is as skimpy and breezy as I can get away with." She gave him a scornful look. "And if you think I can squeeze into anything you own, skinny boy, you should lie down and drink some more water. I think you might be dehydrated. Hallucinating."

He held up both hands placatingly. "Fine, fine. You'll text me if you need me?"

"Reception here is spotty and the Wi-Fi seems overloaded to the point that it's useless—I checked while I was changing. But I'll call the room if there's an emergency. There's probably a house phone downstairs."

Watching her gather her things, he felt a pang of guilt. He shouldn't be abandoning her to her family's machinations. If he were a true friend, he'd be by her side. But facing whatever madcap plan Frances had cooked up felt totally beyond him at the moment, so he let her slip out of the room without another word.

FIVE
Simone

Her outfit was not fine. She'd tried to rally with her sunniest smile and most winning head tilt, but the employee guarding the way to the green didn't even blink. He'd only eyed her chest once before dismissing both it and her. Cleavage was yet another thing not allowed on the golf course. He'd deemed her skirt and shoes passable—with a sniff that told her it was a great concession on his part—but she was required to buy a proper shirt at the pro shop. Until she did, it seemed he was going to physically bar her from entering the course.

She sighed. She was about to own her first polo shirt.

The very large men's shirt was the only one she'd been able to squeeze over her chest. It was snug but workable on her hips and belly, but the rest of the fit was atrocious. The sleeves came down past her elbows in loose, drapey folds. Of course, the tiny section of women's golf shirts mostly came in sizes small and smaller. She eyed herself critically in the bathroom mirror, then pulled out extra hair ties from her purse. Neatly rolling the sleeves up to a more reasonable height on her arms, she wrapped the elastics around the extra fabric and tucked both sides under the cuffs. The shoulder seams were still comically low, but the sleeves now looked purposefully blousy instead of like a child dressing in adult clothes.

She gathered up the cloth hanging past her hips and tied it with yet another elastic, tucking the material right under her breasts. The look was polo crop. She could work with it.

She'd leave the buttons done up until she got past the guard dog at the door and out onto the fairway. With a bit more cleavage and the pop of her lime-green tank showing, she thought the look could be almost cute.

When she arrived, she spotted Gran from across the course, not at all adhering to club rules in her turquoise ensemble, down to her chunky-heeled sandals. No one flouted rules like Gran. She had to respect the player, even if she was still deeply annoyed that she'd been forced to change.

"Darling, whatever are you wearing?" The false laugh that accompanied it tried for coy but was too abrasive to get there.

Simone took that as a sign her polo-crop-chic wasn't working quite as well as she'd hoped. Sighing a micro sigh, she turned toward her aunt, who was swaying toward Simone with a cocktail in hand, rings glinting on every finger. Her gold bracelets clinked as she raised one arm for a standoffish hug, and her air-kiss left enough space to ensure no one's makeup would be endangered.

"Hi, Aunt Mabel." She summoned all the enthusiasm she could, knowing her uncle would be somewhere nearby, scrutinizing her every interaction. If she didn't sparkle to his standards, she'd come home to a strongly-worded email about how she was letting the family business down. It would remind her that he didn't ask much of her: he didn't make her come to shareholder meetings. All he asked was that she employ a little soft diplomacy at their events and schmooze with guests and VIP members.

Mabel brayed another laugh as she gestured at Simone's shirt, narrowly avoiding slopping her cocktail all down its front. "It's certainly a statement, darling. I hope you packed something a little more appropriate for the gala."

"Yes, of course, Auntie M!" She beamed at her aunt as innocently as possible. The nickname was not one Mabel loved, and Simone took a petty sort of pleasure in the other woman's eye twitching in response.

Simone had to hand it to Uncle Dick—he was clear-eyed about his wife's strengths and weaknesses. Her comments were nearly always cutting, her laugh always landed on the side of too loud, and she tended to alienate the wives and girlfriends of the powerful men they were trying to court. Her daughter Sam had no interest in socializing, being strictly focused on the numbers, stats, and contracts side of the business. Gran, as the largest stakeholder and first investor, was indulged and allowed to be as eccentric as she wished. Meanwhile, Simone-the-poor-cousin was trotted out as second string. Not that she could complain, when they'd paid for her fancy private school education and gifted her shares in their development business with only a few strings attached. If those strings sometimes tugged in uncomfortable ways, well, the people who pulled them were still family.

"Your parents are so busy they can't pick up the phone these days? Mark didn't call me to tell me you were engaged. I was quite offended that Mother was the one to tell me. And where is your ring?" One dangerously-tanned, leathery hand extended to reach for Simone's, as though Mabel expected the ring to be produced on the spot.

It was exactly the response she'd expected. Congratulations from Mabel would be unheard of. Not that Simone needed congratulations for a fake engagement, but still, it would have been nice.

"And where is James, speaking of?" Mabel stretched her neck to look around for him. Not finding him, she went back to the topic of her brother, Simone's father, the thorn in her side. "Mark is really something else. You should thank your lucky stars you're an only child, darling." Her rant continued as she turned, seeking James amongst all the reporters and guests. She wasn't letting anyone get a word in anytime soon.

Mabel held a grudge a mile deep against Simone's dad. When Uncle Dick had gone to him for money to start their business, her brother had turned them down, and she was as bitter about it now as she had been twenty years ago. Dad had never been much for speculating. He put in his hours for the hydroelectric company, avoided debt, built his pension, and minded his own business. Against her son's advice, Gran had stepped in to help her son-in-law, cashing out retirement savings in exchange for half the company. Her gamble had paid off, but the choices made all those years ago still rippled through the family.

When Mabel finally turned back to her, Simone cut into her monologue. "Mom and Dad are on vacation right now. They're visiting my Aunt Eloise in Quebec. I'm sure they'll call you when they get back."

She was sure they would not. Dad avoided his sister and brother-in-law as much as possible, and Mom tried to pretend they didn't exist at all.

Mabel was looking at her bare hand again.

"The ring is gorgeous, and I adore it, but I had to get it resized." She nearly winced as she said it. She tried to give her aunt as few openings as possible to comment on her body. Even mentioning her finger size could be enough to travel down an unwanted path.

Thankfully, Mabel didn't pounce: Gran's arrival triggered a fresh round of complaints from her aunt. Simone glared daggers at Gran. Now they both had to listen to how Simone hadn't called her own aunt to tell her the news, and why Mabel was always the last to know anything important. Gran had enough grace to look embarrassed. But only slightly.

"Come now, Mabel, that's enough of your fussing. Kids these days are always sharing their news on social media, but Simone let her grandma be her spokeswoman, and I was honored to do it. Now, are we going to start this opening ceremony, or what?"

Giving her grandmother another speaking look, Simone was about to ask why they were there when she saw the small crowd gathering around the tee-off area. In a crowd of mostly middle-aged men in golf attire, her uncle was chief among them, a lit cigar in one hand and an open cigar box in the other, schmoozing with the VIPs and the press. This was where Simone was likely supposed to be—flashing dimples and cleavage at rich men and making small talk with their much younger wives. Not that Uncle Dick ever told her this explicit job description. He didn't need to. The cues were clear, as were her wardrobe and hair allowance.

Gran caught her arm and began walking her over, the shorter woman dragging Simone down with each step. Simone shook her arm free, irritated.

Gran waved at someone in the distance. "I'll explain everything later. It's nothing to worry about. There's been a little misunderstanding, and it'll all get sorted out in good time." This was muttered under her breath, through a teeth-baring smile. Walking a quarter step behind, she nudged at Simone with one shoulder, herding her grand-daughter where she wanted her to go.

Simone began to feel hounded. Gran was forcing her down a bizarre path without explanation, and she couldn't be sure if anyone had her best interests at heart. Gran loved her, but she'd not think twice about putting Simone in a situation that was awkward or potentially damaging. Hell, she already had! Simone was fake-engaged, for good-ness sake. It was the *why* that was troubling her. Why wouldn't Gran tell her?

A florid man intercepted them when they were nearly at the green. He looked vaguely familiar, but it wasn't until he squinted a leer at Simone's chest that his iden-tity crystallized. The man who'd bumped into her on the dock. Time had not sobered him—either that, or he'd found more alcohol in the interim. She hoped he wouldn't drink himself sick.

"Frances!" Though they were close, the man boomed her grandmother's name like he was calling from across the green. "I never thought I'd see your face again after you lost so badly! If you're here for a rematch, I'm afraid I'd be willing to take your money." He directed another leer at Simone: perhaps it was just his normal expression. "So, this is your beautiful granddaughter. She's just as pretty as her picture. I can't wait to claim my prize." His expression turned absolutely lecherous. Simone shuddered before she could catch herself.

Gran gave a high, false laugh. "Oh Bob, you *rascal*. You know the girl is engaged! I'm sure you got my email. Her fiancé is the jealous sort!" Another trill of amusement. "But I've got my lucky earrings on, and I'm ready for a rematch—whenever you can scrape together enough cash, of course."

Wait, this was about gambling? What was going on?

Uncle Dick finally approached, greeting them all with his best glad-handing routine. "Taggert, you old bastard. It's good to see you." He slapped the man on the shoulder with a cigar still in his hand, then leaned over to give Gran a peck. "Frances, stunning as always." He nodded to Simone. "I see you've already met our firm's most important new partner, Bob Taggert. Simone is my wife's niece."

Bob reached for a cigar from the box Uncle Dick offered and sniffed it appreciatively, still eying Simone over the open lid. She distinctly wished she hadn't undone quite so many of her shirt's buttons. Forcing her expression into a neutral, vapid smile, she pretended she hadn't caught his open ogling. When she looked at Gran, her smile turned pained. She was used to being thrown into potentially uncomfortable situations. But she'd never before felt like she was swimming with sharks.

"Frances tells me the girl is engaged. I don't know about you, Dick, but I don't see a ring on that finger. And from where I stand, that means open season, if you know what I mean." He chuckled dryly and slid sly eyes over to Gran. "I did win the girl fair and square, Frances."

Uncle Dick looked as confused as Simone felt, but recovered quickly, apparently deciding to hear only what he wanted. "Yes, I hear congratulations are in order, Simone. We always wondered when James would man up and get you to settle down." He laughed at his great joke.

Gran tittered perfunctorily, but Simone could only blink. This is what her uncle thought, of her, of James...of relationships? Uncle Dick seemed to take her silence for agreement, taking out the cutter to trim Bob's cigar. The thought of where they could apply that cutter to curb their bullshit popped into her mind and would not leave. She turned to hide her smile.

Bob elbowed Uncle Dick. "The girl plays coy, I see. I like a shy woman. That fiancé shouldn't leave her alone if he wants to keep her." He elbowed Uncle Dick again, who guffawed on cue, taking another puff of his cigar.

"You know, Bob, just the other day I was saying to the Premier over drinks that men have gone soft these days. They don't know how to work hard and go after what they want."

Ah yes—Uncle Dick, the self-made man, if you didn't count his mother-in-law bankrolling his start up. A convenient way to rewrite history.

He snorted and continued. "The Premier couldn't attend this weekend, but I'll arrange for you to meet next month. He was very interested in our development ideas for..."

His voice faded beneath the rushing in Simone's ears. She was going to explode into tiny bits. The rage rose in a wave from her toes to the tops of her ears, her fists clenched and trembling. Her body was going to poof into red mist.

An arm dropped around her gently; her shoulder felt a comforting squeeze. She leaned in automatically before registering who it was, then started back, whipping her head around. James smiled down grimly. He'd heard enough, and he was looking at her like he knew exactly what she was thinking.

She looked into his eyes and knew that, even if he hated this, he'd play along, because he cared about her. He had her back. Her answering smile was a little watery, which crinkled his brow in concern. That tiny crease seemed connected to her heart by a fine string; she'd swear she felt the tug. More tears threatened to rise, an aftereffect of the rage-adrenaline that had been pumping through her, but she blinked them back and turned to the group.

Aunt Mabel, fumes from her cocktail wafting ahead of her, exuberantly greeted James. "Congratulations, James, *darling,*" she drawled. Mabel always fawned over him. He was so tall, so intelligent, and, of course, so *fit.* Aka skinny, a goal Mabel was always chasing. Simone was especially touched that James had received congrats while she, of course, had not.

"So," Bob boomed. "This is the fiancé, is it? Better hang on tight to your little lady, young man. You might lose her otherwise. Women are fickle like that." He chuckled again, sincerely pleased with his own joke, and stuck his hand out. "Bob Taggert."

James removed his arm from around Simone to offer Bob a handshake, one so firm the tendons stood out on the back of his hand. If this was a power play, all these men could go ahead and spare her their bullshit. Now Uncle Dick was slapping his back as James shook his hand and received congratulations for "tying her down." It was all very gross.

If she'd listened to James on the dock, they could be at home right now, making popcorn and settling into a movie marathon. But she had committed to this ridiculous farce, and she would see it through.

The staff member who had been frantically, fruitlessly trying to corral all the guests and press finally approached them. "Please gather for our ceremonial tee-off!"

SIX

James

"**Y**ou okay?" He placed his arm around her again, to give her reassurance and for the pleasure of holding her. A vice he usually didn't allow himself to indulge in. But she probably needed it right now, he thought. As she leaned into him, her sigh told him she felt a measure of safety in his body. He could give her that small comfort.

The group of VIPs, dressed in collared golf shirts, gathered for a picture at the first tee. Press folks and other guests milled around, observing and chatting. One woman with a press lanyard stood a little off to the side, ignoring the drinks and scribbling notes. She looked vaguely familiar. Maybe he'd seen her on the news.

The weekend itinerary he'd found in their room said the first tee-off would start in a few minutes. The VIP groups would go first: it was timed so they would hit the last hole just as the sinking sun started to paint the sky pink.

He supposed it would be romantic, or atmospheric—if you were into that. If you could ignore the water waste, maintenance efforts, and energy consumption that all this artificial beauty required. He shrugged away the thought. His priority was getting them both off this course. At this point, he didn't even care if they couldn't get separate rooms. He didn't care what he might have to say, or pretend, or play along with. He just wanted to get her out.

He positioned them on the far side of the group shot, away from Bob and Dick. Those two could go right to hell, as far as he was concerned.

The fact that Simone was letting him lead her around like a lost puppy worried him. Usually, she took charge in social situations and he followed in her wake. Especially when her family was involved. She always gritted her teeth, plastered on a smile, and expertly guided them both through whatever minefields her family had concocted.

They shuffled around according to the photographer's directions. She was doing her best with an unruly group more concerned with getting to their canapes and cocktails. James obliged her request that he move to the back because of his height, but he made sure to nudge Simone so she was right in front of him. He was not letting her out of his sight while they were in this place.

She reached back for him; he wrapped his fingers around hers without a second thought. She really must have been shaken by that gross dude. Or maybe by the way

Frances had very obviously thrown her granddaughter to the wolves without a second thought. The minute he got Frances alone, they were going to have some words. Strong ones.

The photographer moved them along, cracking jokes and coaxing smiles until they'd arrived at the end of the process with surprisingly little fuss. The mayor of the nearest town gave a speech about grand partnerships and mutual friendships and what a great honor it was to open the course. You could practically see the dollar signs in the man's eyes as he spoke, and James had to wonder what kind of personal kickbacks he'd received from the deal. He still hadn't talked to Simone about the articles he'd found about land rights. Now, that was going to be a thorny conversation. Maybe he'd wait till they got home.

The mayor wound down his speech. Dick and Bob stepped up to cut the ribbon together, then posed for another picture, cigars temporarily set aside. It was impressive that Bob was still upright, never mind that he still possessed the manual dexterity to operate scissors. He didn't seem to have slowed down since they'd first met on the dock.

Once the little ceremony was over and they'd all politely clapped on cue, he and Simone began edging back toward the resort, needing only a glance at each other to reach perfect understanding. They both wanted out, and they were in this together. Her hand was still anchored to his.

They were nearly at the path back to the lodge when Mabel and her daughter Sam intercepted them. Sam was even smiling as she approached, an expression that, in Sam's case, was about the same thing as an effusive squeal of glee.

"Mother tells me congratulations are in order. I wish you both every happiness." All said very formally, but that small smile conveyed genuine warmth.

Simone finally released James's hand to give her cousin a brief, tight hug. Sam looked very much like her mother, sharing Mabel's light skin and rosy cheeks, short brown hair, and petite frame, but without her nose job and dangerous tan.

Sam had always been nice enough to him, but she was even more introverted than he was. Whenever he and Sam were left alone without Simone to carry the conversation, they ended up standing awkwardly beside each other until one of them left, mumbling an excuse.

Mabel cut in on the cousins' reunion. "Darling, I've had the most *wonderful idea*. You can do your engagement pictures at the resort! Then we'll be able to use them for promotional images. You know, we plan to be *the* spot for weddings." Mabel clutched at his arm. She often spoke in italics, but she didn't usually bother to be affectionate with him. It was odd to see her being so ingratiating—he'd always had the distinct impression she thought he was stuffy and boring.

Simone, probably still reeling from his earlier outburst, was already marshaling excuses for the two of them, obviously trying to spare him from dealing with her family. He didn't know how to tell her that while he'd been sitting in their fancy hotel room, recovering from his headache and actively missing her, all his anger had drained away.

He'd realized, back in that room, that his overwhelming emotion had been worry. Worry for her, and worry for the way Simone's family kept using her. The package that had been left there was enough to worry anyone. He'd decided that he was going to be there for her, no matter what. He'd changed clothes, downed a scalding cup of coffee, and arrived at the green just in time. He only wished he'd been faster.

"Aunt Mabel, James is tired from the drive, and we're going to get a friend to take pictures for us later. You don't need to bother the photographer."

"*Nonsense,* darling." An emphatic wave of her fresh cocktail slopped over the brim of the glass. "Lana would be *thrilled* to take some romantic photos, I'm sure."

"I think she went with the golfers, mother," Sam interjected, raising an eyebrow at Simone. She clearly didn't know what was going on, but had picked up on the undercurrents.

"Oh, she'll be back in a few minutes. *Christina*!" She yelled the name at the top of her lungs. James flinched, taking a half-step backwards before he could catch himself.

A competent-looking black-haired young woman, wearing thick-framed glasses and sharply-pressed golf clothes, rushed toward them with a clipboard. "Yes, Mrs. Montgomery?" She was obviously used to being screamed for, but she paused with a genuine smile when she saw Simone. "Oh hi, Ms. Larson. I hadn't seen you yet. Glad you could make it."

Simone smiled back. "Good to see you again, Christina. Please, call me Simone. This is…James." He noted the pause. While they might be playing along with whatever was happening today, she was apparently not ready to call him her fiancé outright.

"Darling, don't be shy. He's her *fiancé*, Christina. And I want to set up an engagement shoot with Lana. They'll take photos on the green now, and they can take some in formal wear before the gala tomorrow. Oh! They should showcase the grounds for the brochure—maybe even something by the pool." She eyed Simone critically, as though rethinking her last suggestion.

James suppressed an eyeroll. Simone didn't react. He knew she was completely used to her aunt's small digs at her expense. James still wished she'd say something to the woman's rudeness, but, as usual, he took his cues from her. She reached for his hand again and he threaded their fingers together, running his thumb down the side of hers soothingly.

He'd never before appreciated how wonderful it was to hold hands, to be reached for, to provide and receive comfort with a simple touch. It was bliss.

"But Aunt Mabel, I don't have my ring. Remember? It's being resized. I just couldn't do an engagement shoot without it," Simone said, tone dripping with honey. She practically batted her eyes.

James cleared his throat. The box in his pocket was suddenly heavy. Simone looked up at him through long lashes. "What?" She murmured it low enough that Mabel might not have heard.

He wrapped an arm around her as an excuse to get close enough that only she would hear what he was about to whisper. "Um. There was a ring. It was waiting in the hotel room."

She looked at him uncomprehendingly. Either she hadn't heard, or she didn't understand.

"Speak up, James, darling." Mabel had come even close, trying to hear.

He froze, uncertain of which way to play this—he hated thinking under pressure. Simone was still staring at him blankly.

Almost on autopilot, he reached into his pocket and pulled out the little velvet box. Time stopped. He knew it must have, because everyone stopped moving. And stared at them. All eyes were on the blue box in his hand. How could a tiny thing weigh so much?

Christina broke the spell by squealing, making both Simone and Sam jump.

"I wanted it to be a surprise. The ring came back from the jeweler right before we left." That was the best he could improvise on the spot, and *damn* Frances for putting him in this position. He didn't even know if it would fit.

Simone seemed to be in a trance. But he had to keep going if he wanted to salvage this. His hand skated from her shoulders down her arm, reaching for her limp fingers. He struggled with the ring box one-handed but finally managed to prize it apart without letting go of her, until it finally opened to reveal a sapphire ring. She gasped.

"It's Gran's ring." She was staring at him in bewilderment. It wasn't the best response if they were supposed to have done this before.

Thankfully, Mabel was too affronted to notice. "Well! She could have at least *asked* if Sam wanted to use it. She does have two granddaughters. *Mother!*" She shrieked over her shoulder.

Sam placed a restraining hand on her arm. "Mom, I'm very happy for Simone to have it. Blue isn't my color, anyway."

That was enough to calm Mabel. "Of course, you're right, my dear. Diamonds are the *only* choice. Colored stones are so old-fashioned."

Through it all, James only had eyes for Simone. She was still searching his face for an answer to a question he couldn't decipher. He tried to tell her silently that he was fine, that he was with her for whatever she needed. She suddenly nodded, her eyes relit by their usual spark, which filled him with relief.

She raised her hand for him, for the ring. Slowly, dreamily. His heart pounded in his chest and drummed in his ears. His palms had gone clammy. They were really doing this.

SEVEN
Simone

It fit. It fit perfectly. She couldn't parse her feelings about any of it: the ring, the fake engagement situation, her family, or, most crucially of all, her feelings about James. But she kept staring at the ring she'd seen so many times before in her grandmother's jewelry box, which somehow looked so different sparkling on her hand in the bright light of day. She glanced at it in between the pictures the photographer took of their hands folded together. Yes, it was her hand wearing that beautiful, uncannily familiar white gold ring: its paired bands interlocking in sweeping curves; its two circular diamonds flanking the large round center sapphire. His long fingers wound around hers, deft and precise with every movement. The pictures would be beautiful. No one else would see the tension Simone noticed in his jaw.

She traced a finger soothingly up one of the raised tendons on his arm. It flattened under her touch, and his hand relaxed ever so slightly.

No matter what happened later, today was a small miracle: she'd been allowed inside those ever-present walls of his. He'd opened a gate for her and locked it behind her, shutting the world away. It was not something she'd ever take for granted. She couldn't help but pet him, just a little, since she so rarely had that pleasure.

The photographer Lana, after she'd finished taking pictures of their hands and the ring in various poses, set them up for the next shot. The sun hid momentarily behind fluffy white clouds, giving them temporary relief from harsh light and deep shadows.

"Okay, we'll take a few with the green in the background. The light's great right now." Lana checked them through her lens, adjusted her camera settings, then stared at the preview screen after taking a few snaps. Meanwhile, Simone and James stood in place, immobile and staring straight ahead. Simone fought down giggles over the absurdity of this whole situation, trying not to fiddle with the ring that would only be on her finger temporarily, not wanting to make things more awkward for James than they already were. She didn't dare look at him.

"All right, you two! Don't be shy, let's see a pose together—like you like each other!" Lana raised her camera in their direction again.

"Sorry, Lana, we're not very comfortable with pictures." If Simone were alone, she'd be working her angles with the best of them. Posing with James was another thing entirely.

"No problem; no problem. Lots of couples are camera-shy. I'll help you out. We'll talk it through. James, why don't you turn to Simone, put your arms around her, and tell me what you thought about her the day you first met. Simone, you can keep your body facing me, but look up at James." A few clicks flashed by her peripheral vision. "Perfect. Now, James, I'd love to hear it. I can tell it's going to be juicy."

He laughed first, and the camera clicked away through that too, through his private smirk of remembrance. She looked up at him and her lips quirked with delight, knowing exactly what he was going to say. Suddenly it was the most natural thing in the world to have his long arms loosely circling her waist, to lean her shoulder against his chest, and to look up into his laughing eyes, lit up behind the wire frames of his glasses.

"The first time we met, Simone was covered in mud and demanding I help her hide in my backyard. I had no idea what was going on and hid with her in my treehouse. I thought we were in danger, maybe from a bear, or a bully, or who knows what. My imagination was running wild with murderers and wild animals." He chuckled again, and it loosened something in her chest. "It turned out it was a game of sardines, and the only danger she was in was not winning."

Lana laughed appreciatively as she kept them moving, posing them in front of views featuring picturesque trees or flowering shrubbery. She was so good at keeping them talking and laughing as they reminisced about pranks and old playmates. Although Simone was standing with her arms looped high around James's neck while his hands rested on her hips, they hadn't returned to their earlier awkwardness.

But as one particular memory faded from both of their lips, she realized that her breasts were pressed up against his chest. Their faces were close enough that the smallest movement would bring them together. His eyes had gone focused and serious, his hands increasingly firm on her hips, until she wasn't sure if he was going to pull her closer or push her away.

Her lips parted, but she couldn't think of what to say to shift the sudden tension. His eyes flicked down, his gaze abruptly hard and bright, shifting back to hers so quickly she could have almost imagined it never left. The clicks of the camera shutter faded in her ears, until all she could hear was her pulse thrumming louder and louder as they stood there, staring.

His face was as familiar to her as her own, yet somehow new and fascinating, transformed by the intensity of his expression. His lashes were long, nearly brushing his glasses, but he'd barely blinked in the moments since they'd pressed their bodies together. She was entranced. Would his expression shift into new territory if she raised her hand to the curls of his auburn hair, stirred by the gentle summer breeze? Or if she touched her nose to his, nuzzling against him, inviting something more? She wanted to see what would come over his expression if she arched up into him, inviting him to run his hands over her with the press of her body, to explore, to taste.

She bit her lip. Her hands were cramping with the continual effort of twining them around his neck—she had to restrain herself from gliding them over his shoulders—and when she wasn't pressed up against him, her body ached with absence. She should step away now before it got even more difficult.

"How about a kiss, you two?" The camera clicks reentered Simone's awareness. Lana made the suggestion quietly, seemingly sensitive to the moment unfolding between them, but James tensed under her hands.

He was looking at her mouth again, making her breath catch. Slowly, his eyes raised to hers. He lifted a questioning brow, which was so quintessentially James that she couldn't help the slow smile that spread in response. Still very serious, he gave a short nod, then leaned closer, bending his neck to reach her.

She met him with the smile still on her lips, unable to hold back a sigh. It felt so natural to press her mouth to his, to shift until they fit together *just right*. All the years that they could have been kissing stretched behind them like a wasteland. What had they been doing all this time? Why hadn't it been *this*? This press of sun-warmed skin; this mouth, alternately soft and firm under hers. His breath coming in short bursts, chest heaving and hands gentle; his touches straining to reach, then melting into hers. Her lip between his teeth was finally where it was supposed to be, and his mouth was meant to tease and suck hers, making its fullness even plumper. This was everything she'd ever wanted to do. She licked at his top teeth, wanting to be inside him, wanting him inside her, needing so much more. Plastering herself against his body, she begged for pressure, for weight, for the proof that he needed her too.

He stiffened. Then withdrew, dropping his hand from where it cradled the back of her head, and catching it in her hair, where it stuck. They spent an awkward moment disentangling while her cheeks burned with shame. She had taken it too far.

She tried to meet his eyes, wanting to make sure he was okay. He was taking great interest in the scenery, hands deep in his pockets, flushing from his high cheekbones to the tips of his ears.

"That was amazing. I got some great shots—you're going to love them." Lana, hurrying over, excitedly gestured to the photo preview. Simone took the camera, giving James a minute to get control of that blush, which was quickly heading into tomato territory.

The tiny picture she saw could have been displayed in a gallery under the title "Lust." She hadn't known her face could look so sensual. Their lips were a whisper apart, and the longing there was something extraordinary. If she hadn't known, she would have said these two people were lovers. Asked about their relationship, she'd have speculated that the anticipation of being together got these two through every moment they were apart. The pang this gave her was something like sadness. Tears threatened her eyes, but she blinked them away and mustered a smile.

"You do beautiful work, Lana." She gestured at James. "We've both had a long day and I know you're being run off your feet this weekend. Should we call it quits for now?"

"Yes, I'll let you go. I'm going to take a dinner break, then head over to the eighteenth hole and get some shots while the light is still good."

Simone checked her watch, surprised to see it was already dinnertime. Free room service was sounding better and better. Lana gathered her extra camera bag from under a tree and waved goodbye, leaving them alone with each other. James still hadn't said anything other than a polite thanks to Lana. She didn't know what he was thinking.

"I still haven't had a chance to corner Gran, and I don't know where she's run off to. I'll have to leave a note for her at the reception desk or something. Cell reception is terrible out here." He didn't meet her eyes to acknowledge what she'd said: he was still staring out at the green as though it had answers only he could see. "I could hunt down Sam and ask if she'll share her room with me. If I can't find Gran."

He looked at her then. "Sam has such a hard time sleeping, she didn't even do sleepovers with you, if I remember correctly. I think she has enough anxiety without us adding to it." He did know too much about her; he knew about her entire family. It was inconvenient. "And last I heard, Mrs. Larson has one of those machines for sleep apnea. I don't think you want to try to sleep through that."

"I don't know what you want me to do, then. I'm trying to find a solution."

"I know you are. I think you should just stay in the room. There's a king bed. We could sleep in it without even seeing each other, there's so much room. It's like an ocean of bed."

She snorted. "I don't know about that, but I guess we could build a pillow barrier. What if I want to take a bath tonight? Would that bother you?"

"Of course not. You can turn into a mermaid like in Splash, and I won't judge." He smirked. And just like that, he was back to normal and everything was fine again, to Simone's great relief. They headed back to the lodge, still riffing on Splash, which they'd watched together for the first time while doing a classic rom-com movie marathon: Hanks edition.

Simone had always adored swimming, the freedom of floating, the way the water cradled and challenged her. She could spend hours in chilly lakewater and barely notice the time passing. James always had to return to shore when he got too cold, warming up in the sun to recover from the frigid water. He sadly didn't have enough body fat to float, either: she'd shake her head in pity whenever he made an attempt. When they'd seen Splash, he'd had his aha moment—she was a mermaid, obviously.

She missed his arm around her. She'd only had the sunshine of his constant attention and affection for a few short hours, but she was already deprived without it. It was silly to get used to it, and even sillier to wish she'd have a reason to touch him. And monumentally stupid to hope that they'd run into someone like Bob again, who might bring out James's protective side. Rightly so—their last encounter with that man had left her shaking and furious. It wasn't worth getting harassed just to return James' attention to her.

She would have to hope that their next engagement photoshoot would give her an excuse to put her hands on him again. If she was very lucky, she might even glimpse that look in his eye once more. And as for the kissing...she dared not hope that he'd ever be willing to do it again.

EIGHT

James

Sharing a room with Simone was going to be a special kind of torture. And he had only himself to blame. She'd offered him an out. More than one. And he hadn't taken it. He hadn't wanted to. He'd convinced her it would be fine, while inwardly shouting to himself that it was a mistake.

She was in the bath while he waited for their room service order. It was best not to think of what she was doing in there, either. No matter how fancy the hotel, bathroom doors were never soundproof. The splashing, humming, and the low murmur of Simone talking to herself—she was always talking to herself—were as clear as though he were in there with her.

It was getting harder to deny that with her was exactly where he wanted to be. He'd thought he finally had that all under control. But that kiss today...it had been monumental. Cataclysmic. Earth-shaking, world-ending. He'd surfaced from it expecting to see the ground rocking under his feet, but instead, the gentle breeze still rippled through the leaves, and the birds were still singing. Simone had kept on with her bright chatter. The only one affected had been him. As usual.

He was the world's biggest sucker, because all he wanted was to do it again.

For all the faults he'd found with the hotel, room service was so prompt that Simone had to cut her bath short. The tub drained noisily enough to be heard through the door, and while Simone toweled herself off in there—not that he was thinking of that—he had time to arrange their plates on the coffee table and settle onto the couch. He scrolled through the movie channels while he waited, looking for the least sexy option. Something with a lot of bros being bros and gross-out humor. It wasn't what they usually watched together, but he needed a serious distraction to shift his mental state.

Simone finally emerged. When he saw her, he realized he'd made a strategic error. He should have been steeling himself to see her fresh out of the bath. *Mayday. The mermaid has absconded with the captain's wits.*

She was in what he could only assume were pajamas, though they certainly didn't make him feel sleepy. Her satiny pink shorts were cut high, showing off the sweep of her dimpled, rounded thighs. Her cheeks glowed pink.

And she seemed moist all over. Lickable. Every part of her was fascinating, down to her thick, shapely calves and pretty painted toes. There was no safe place to look.

This was ridiculous. He saw her legs all the time. This was no big deal. If only he could tear his eyes away for a moment, he'd prove it to himself.

She was wearing a hoodie over a satin tank which matched her shorts, but hadn't zipped it all the way up. The lacy edge of the tank and two smooth, thin straps were visible. God help him if she ever took that hoodie off. No evidence of a bra, again. He had to stop himself from speculating about her undergarment situation. Two slow sweeps up and down her body were two too many.

She was looking at the TV menu without seeming to notice him staring. "The Hangover? Ugh. No thanks."

Plopping down beside him, she held out her hand for the remote. He thrust it at her, then took the lid off his plate just for something to do. There was too much skin beside him, too much light, fresh scent overwhelming his senses. It was familiar, but he'd never experienced it fresh out of the shower. It reminded him of sitting on a patio at sunset—he could almost see the golden light washing over her face as she squeezed a lime wedge into her cocktail, the mist from the rind sharp in the soft evening air. Citrus and faint floral and bees humming in the distance.

She muttered and scrunched her face as she scrolled through the channels, completely ignoring her food, as usual. He was already halfway through his burger, and she was still flipping through the options.

He cleared his throat. "You should eat, Simone. Just put anything on for now and we'll change it later." He hadn't meant to sound scolding, but she glanced over with a disapproving expression. She didn't like to be told what to do, and he expected a set-down for it.

Instead, she gave a secretive, baffling little smile as she clicked the channel button one last time. He narrowed his eyes, turning back to the TV, then groaned when he saw her pick. Magic Mike XXL. The movie had already started, but she didn't seem to care.

He returned to his burger in resignation. She might be unaffected by this afternoon, but these were exactly the kind of horny vibes he had been hoping to avoid.

"Ooh, I love this part." She was smiling over the first bite of her Thai-inspired dish, holding her chopsticks to her lips with her eyes glued to the screen.

"Is it Tatum Channing or Channing Tatum? I don't think either is a real first or last name." Onscreen, Mike was trying to convince a scantily clad Jada Pinkett Smith to give him a shot at dancing.

She shushed him with an airy wave of her chopsticks. The open delight in her expression as she picked at her peppers and watched Tatum gyrating upside down in front of a woman in the club was baffling. He caught up the remote and paused it.

"What about this is sexy? The man is on his head right now. He looks ridiculous." James gestured at the screen.

She laughed at him, leaning over to steal a fry off his plate. "Yeah, I mean, that part is a little extra. But the implication is that he's willing to go out of his way to go down. It's all about showing off what this man would do to please you if he were with you. Plus, it's fun, and I see nothing wrong with that." She gestured impatiently at the remote, so he hit play.

Her delight continued. She giggled at the part where Cheesy-Taters or whatever his name was used two women as a tabletop to writhe on. She smirked when the scene ended with him face-down between a pair of thighs.

When the guys on screen left the club a few minutes later, she looked over thoughtfully. "Sex is sort of...well, I mean it's great, but it can be awkward and silly, too. That's part of why having a sense of humor about yourself is so sexy. It signals that Mike is what you might call 'good, giving, and game.' Don't you think?"

He scrubbed his hands through his hair. Now they were talking about this subject? In years of friendship, they'd never gone there. She didn't realize he *couldn't* talk to her about this. It made him panicky to even think about it. He searched for a different track of conversation.

"I don't think that's the takeaway from this movie. Come on, it's about oiled-up men with fake tans and abs dancing around. It's superficial shit."

She pursed her lips, obviously ready to disagree.

His heart was racing, and she was gearing up for a pleasant debate. He stood abruptly. "I'm going to take a shower. I'll leave you to it."

He stayed in the bathroom as long as he could, standing under the spray while the water numbed and soothed, until his guilt over water waste made him turn it off. When he reemerged, she'd moved to the bed. The TV was on some sort of landscaping show, which was probably a peace offering—a neutral choice that would prompt no awkward conversation.

He climbed into his side of the bed. The room was cool enough that the covers were comforting rather than stifling. Simone had placed a line of pillows down the center: it was the clear boundary he needed. When he peered over the small mountain range separating them, she was already half-asleep, her long lashes making slow sweeps as she blinked heavily. Reaching over, he plucked the remote from her limp hand, turning off the TV and room lights.

"Goodnight," he whispered. Then lay awake for hours, listening to her slow, even breaths.

The next morning, he rose while she was still asleep, shifting her soft, warm arm off his chest and moving as quietly as possible through the dark room. The pillow barrier hadn't made much difference. Simone was a snuggler. He wrote a hasty note for her in the too-bright glare of the bathroom lights. He'd left his running clothes out on top of his suitcase the night before. A run would help clear his head, even if it was indoors. He didn't want to go far, or blunder into bears on a trail he didn't know, but a hotel treadmill would do the job.

Two miles in, he was starting to feel clear and light, his mind finally quiet as he listened to nothing but the pulse pounding in his ears. Then he saw her in the mirror, the only other person in that surprisingly spacious gym.

"You could have woken me, you know."

He slowed to a pace where he could talk. "You looked peaceful. It was such a long day, it's good you got some extra rest." He knew she was usually up at dawn to open the shelter. There were animals to feed and a long list of tasks to start.

She yawned and stretched with a cute little sigh that made him smile, even as he shook his head. "You could have kept sleeping," he teased.

"It'll be better once I start moving. It's going to be another long day, and I want to talk to you about it."

Picking the treadmill next to him, she started walking, slowly at first. She was wearing the same lime-green exercise outfit from yesterday, its complicated chest straps stretching and contracting with every bounce. He nearly tripped face-first, grabbing the machine's handles to steady himself. Right. Eyes up.

The mirror reflected her raised eyebrows, along with the puzzled look on her sleepy face. He wasn't usually clumsy. Thankfully, she didn't question him about his sudden case of two left feet.

"So, are we leaving after breakfast?" He couldn't quite keep the plea out of his tone.

"Nice try. I have to do this." She upped her speed. "J, I've been thinking. You should go. This is my thing, and I shouldn't have dragged you into this nightmare. If you go home today, I can think up an excuse. I'm sure I can catch a ride home with Sam, or maybe Gran." She looked doubtful, rightfully so, because those two were chronically hard to pin down, each in their own particular way.

"I'm staying. There's no way I'm going to leave you with these people. And I'll go along with this whole thing if it will make you happy. But you and your grandmother need to have a serious talk when you get home. I don't know what she's playing at, but it sucks, Simone."

"Oh, you know Gran. She probably just got in over her head. I'm sure there's an explanation." She bit her lip. "She always means well."

Her blind spot was a mile across. Frances did *not* mean well, as far as he was concerned. But the day that Simone admitted it would be the day his dad finally stopped drinking. And as far as James could tell, that day would never come.

He sighed. "What's the plan for today, then?"

It turned out the plan was to be seen together at every possible location on the island. Mabel had asked Christina, assisted by the entire hotel events team, to coordinate a resort tour, complete with appointments at photoshoot locations. It was choreographed down to the minute: Christina must have been up very early putting it all together. He could have pitied her, if he weren't the one abiding by her schedule.

It wasn't as difficult as it should have been to play the doting fiancé. Holding Simone's hand, his thumb brushing over that pretty blue-stoned ring, hiding his smirk as she made up details on the spot about their imagined wedding, discussing options for decorating and table arrangements—it was all surprisingly easy.

Their wedding promised to be beautiful. Riotous color in all the décor, specialty cocktails, magically lit centerpieces, a live band for dancing long into the night, and at least three flavors of cake. Sounded like a real party. Too bad none of them would get to see it.

Their photoshoot by the pool was more difficult, as he tried not to ogle her bright red, high-waisted retro bathing suit. Thankfully, the photographer didn't ask for anything too intimate, posing them side-by-side on deck chairs un-der the late-June sun. He opted for a mocktail, and she sipped a cocktail as they lounged, looking at each other adoringly. Sunglasses were necessary—less for the sun than to blunt her impact on his eyes. Lana asked if they want-ed to do anything in the water, but Simone claimed she wanted to keep her hair dry. She had artfully arranged it in hot-iron curls that had taken her a while to do, but he knew it must be an excuse. Simone always chose the water over her hair, no matter how fancily it was done up.

He was grateful she'd opted out. There was no doubt in his mind that being in the water together would have inspired the photographer to get them much closer. He banished the thought of kissing water droplets off Simone's lips, along with the feeling of her wet body pressed against him.

By the time they were back in their room to change for the gala, he was wrung out. Just a few more hours, and they could escape back to their little haven. He was starting to like their hotel room a whole lot. He liked it more than any other room in the entire resort, which he could now say with certainty because he'd seen nearly all of them.

Simone showered first, waltzing in and out of the bathroom with a cute old-fashioned shower cap covering her head. As she pinned up her curled hair, she sat at the desk in front of the mirror wearing only her robe, its silk still damply clinging to her skin. The only way to stop himself from going over there to check whether she had anything on beneath that robe, was to escape into the bathroom. The mirror had fogged over from her shower, and, defying the bathroom fan running at full power, her lime mojito fragrance hung thickly in the air.

His shower was as cold as he could stand it.

NINE
Simone

Getting dolled up was second nature to her, but it never stopped being a hell of a lot of work. She had touched up her curls with a few licks of her iron, pinning them into an artful updo that she thought struck a balance between haphazard and sleek. Her gown's fitted, sparkly V-neck bodice dipped low, its deep-blue chiffon skirt forming a light cloud around her. She couldn't help but twirl in front of the mirror, admiring the way the skirt's top layer momentarily floated in the air, making her feel one step from dancing. The best part about this dress was that she could wear a proper plunge bra and didn't need any shapewear to smooth out the lines.

She felt like a princess as they made their way down to the gala. All she was missing was the tiara. It wasn't a fantasy she usually wanted for herself, but on the arm of the man beside her, it was irresistible.

"Have I mentioned how sharp you look tonight?" She smiled up at him teasingly, just to see his eyes roll exaggeratedly as he looked down at her with a barely hidden smile.

"Only five times, but you can always tell me again." His tone was both long-suffering and secretly pleased, which made her grin brighter. "If you need to swoon, just give me a heads up."

It was easier to make it a joke, rolling her own eyes in response. If she didn't, she might have told him he made her knees weak, and that, when he'd come out of the bathroom in his dress shirt, fussing with the cufflinks, she'd caught her breath.

She'd let him sort out his sleeves himself, and tie his tie, because she didn't trust herself to have her hands on him. James in everyday clothes was a pleasure—the long lines of him, the way his clothing draped enticingly over his torso. In a suit, he was devastating.

They walked into the ballroom hand in hand. Somewhere in the course of the day, traipsing between photo ops and facility tours, reaching for his hand had become as natural as breathing. He was hers for tonight, within the confines of this little farce, and she reveled in the fact, in ways that continued to surprise her.

It felt like a simulation of freefall. In VR goggles, where she could pretend that the wind was rushing past her face and that her parachute was waiting for her: all of the adrenaline, none of the risk. Nothing she said or did tonight would count in the real world, because they both knew this was all pretend. Their friendship would still be intact when it ended. Nothing she said or did within *reason*, she cautioned herself. She couldn't push this heady euphoria too far. She still had to face him on the other side of tonight.

They found their assigned table on the seating chart, but before they could make their way over, Christina, magnificent in a body-con black dress, intercepted them. "Lana is waiting for you on the front steps. She wants to get shots of you dressed up while the light is still good." She shooed them out of the ballroom and went back to her clipboard.

James sighed next to her, and she internally echoed him. That damn clipboard had ruled their whole day. She was beginning to feel hounded, and briefly indulged in the fantasy of a clipboard-burning party. She would dance victoriously around the fire, screaming at it to die, James watching from a safe distance with crossed arms, his expression either amused or disturbed, she couldn't tell which. It was her fantasy: she should have been able to dictate how he would respond, but he defied her expectations even there.

Grumpy now, she grabbed his hand and pulled him toward the front entrance. "Let's get this over with."

"How romantic," he drawled, keeping up easily with his long, ground-eating strides. "You sure do sweep me off my feet."

"Hush." They stepped outside together.

The light was beautiful. Its sunset glow transformed the log cabin exterior, which had looked so gaudy in the afternoon: now it gleamed softly off the gold embellishments. Lana directed them to stand next to a gilded pillar. She took a few shots of them leaning against it, looking moodily into the middle distance, then a few more, staring moodily down the camera lens. Moodiness was the key to what Lana called a "model pose." Simone wasn't sure what use these shots were for the resort's publicity, which she figured should be sunny smiles and euphoric golfers, but Lana was the one with the vision. This time around, it was even more effortless to be comfortable around Lana, natural with the camera, and to feel like she belonged in James's personal space.

Too soon, Lana released them, saying she wanted to get a few more angles of the exterior.

There had to be some way of stretching their moment alone. She nudged James with an elbow. "Let's go see the sunset over the lake. It won't take long."

He ambled alongside her down the winding path, steadying her with a hand on her arm when her heels wobbled in the gaps of the stone path. She beamed gratefully at him. Trailing a finger down her arm, he took her hand in his, clasping it firmly.

"My prince," she teased.

"The fancy getup is slowing you down, Larson. Normally I'd be hustling to catch up."

"Next time I'll wear the tux and flats. You can wear the dress and heels and see how you do. I'd rock your look without breaking a sweat."

"Pass." He lifted their joined hands. "I'll stick with gallant support system."

Her breath caught as they emerged through the trees: the huge golden sun was hanging low in the sky, shimmering a path on the rippling lake.

"It's so beautiful."

"Best thing we've seen all day." James helped her onto the smaller floating dock, where she narrowly avoided catching a heel between the boards.

"I should just take the damn things off."

"Here," James nudged her closer. "I'll stand over the space."

She found her equilibrium on the gently rocking surface, his body behind her and his hand loosely resting on her hip. It was a pose they'd done all day: right now, it felt instinctive.

James leaned closer, his suit jacket brushing her shoulders. His nose grazed the top of her ear.

"Have I told you that you smell like a lime cocktail?"

Simone held back a squeak, trying for a nonchalant laugh. "Cocktails aren't exactly your favorite thing. It's just my lotion."

"Mmm..." His breath was warm on the side of her neck, and she tilted her head in silent invitation. "I don't mind them on you."

"Is that so?" Her brain was short-circuiting.

He nuzzled gently into the crook of her neck, then inhaled. Goosebumps flowed down her spine from that small point of contact. "It's different here. Spicier."

"That's my perfume. Different base notes." Stringing sentences together was getting harder. Her arched neck begged for his mouth. "I think they make a candle if you like it."

He huffed quietly against her skin. She might have whimpered.

"Somehow, I don't think that would be the same." He finally seemed to notice her silent cues. "Was there something else you wanted?"

"Me?" She swallowed and tried again. "No. I mean, whatever you want is fine with me."

"Well." He traveled upward to nuzzle gently at her hair-line. "If it's a matter of what I *want*, that changes every-thing." His lips pressed softly behind her ear and fogged her mind. She definitely whimpered that time.

Wait, what? She tried to turn into him, but his hands were still on her hips. Her attempt only managed to push one shoulder more firmly against him. What did he want, and how did that change things? She craned her head back, searching for his face.

"What do you mean?" His eyes would tell her. He had never been able to lie to her.

"I'll tell you later. We're canoodling, remember?"

She snorted and turned forward. "If you insist. Just try not to get too carried away."

"Hmm. Maybe you're the one who needs to remember not to get carried away." He murmured that last into the curve of her neck, right where it met her shoulder, lips touching her skin. She shivered.

"That's an interesting reaction." His tone was musing, but his hands flexed on her hips. "I'll tell you something I *want*. I would like to bite you right there." His mouth brushed her neck once more. "What do you think of that?"

This shouldn't be turning her on, but it most definitely was. She tried for airy and aloof. "If that's really what you want, I suppose you could. Not too hard, though, and no marks. They wouldn't go with my dress." This was the most ridiculous conversation they'd ever had, and she was breathless with anticipation.

He laughed darkly. "I disagree, but as you wish."

She thought she was ready for this. It should have been like any other kiss. But nothing could have prepared her for the scrape of his teeth against the tendons of her neck and the soft nips he trailed across her shoulder. His hands left her hips to sweep up her sides and back in a slow, measured caress. And she could do nothing but melt back against him, lifting her chin to rest her head against his shoulder, not caring if it destroyed her careful updo, giving him all the access he needed. Anything he wanted. At that moment, she would have let him take her apart and put her back together without a word of protest.

He was at the crook of her neck again, biting the tiniest fraction harder, testing her until she moaned and pressed up against him encouragingly. Between gentle bites, he whispered approval, his tempo growing frantic: then a pause, followed by a soft, obscene suck right behind her ear, exactly where her blood was pounding. She was on fire. If this man didn't satisfy her soon, she was going to...

"Oh my god, this is perfect!" Lana's voice interrupted. "You two against the sunset are the most gorgeous silhouette. I can't believe I didn't think of coming down here.

Just hold that for a minute." The camera clicked away as they stayed painfully frozen.

Lana, oblivious, hurried back to them while checking her preview screen. "Damn, you're so hot together. I can't wait to send you these after I'm done editing. You're going to love them." She checked her watch. "I need to get inside and shoot the VIPs. I'll see you in there!" She hurried off, leaving them standing awkwardly separate, hands to themselves.

Simone cleared her throat and willed her swollen tongue to work. "Was that what you wanted, then?" A sidelong glance told her he was rigid with disapproval, which he only ever was when she had fucked up something badly. Well, he could take his disapproval and shove it. He was the one who had started kissing up on her. This was not her problem. She carefully turned on her heel and marched back up the path without another word.

TEN

James

He'd fucked it all up badly, judging by the stiff way she stalked ahead of him. When he contrasted it with the way she'd been in his arms—pliant, fluid, soft—it was all the more clear. He laughed inwardly, bitterly, without even a hint of amusement. What had he been thinking? She'd asked him what he wanted, and he'd just...told her. And then did exactly what he liked. When had he ever done that before? He cast back into his childhood memories, but not a single example came to mind. What he wanted had never been important.

Except to Simone. He knew she cared about what was important to him, but she'd never before asked him outright. And then she suddenly expected him to voice something he could hardly even admit to himself. And he had. He'd opened his mouth and let it all fall out. Something about the entire situation: her constant proximity, her continual touch, the temporary permission he had to claim her as his, had made him lose his careful safeguards.

How often had he thought about that graceful curve of her neck, the round smoothness of her shoulder? How often had he wanted to sink into her and never resurface? Too often for sanity. Too often for easy friendship. Now that he knew how soft her skin was, the noises she made when he touched her, the way she'd seemed as entranced by him as he was with her, he didn't know if he could ever recover. He didn't know if he wanted to.

He caught up to Simone in time to pull out her chair before she sat down. Maybe it was formal of him, but her family and any guests watching would appreciate the gesture. In response, she gave a small snort, obviously still frustrated with him.

They had the questionable honor of sitting at one of the VIP tables. James noted their old friend Bob with dismay: he was making quite the fashion statement by pairing his suit with a Stetson and a bolero tie, and even more unfortunately, was also heading towards the VIP table. Too late, he saw the man's place card was right next to Simone's.

Bob turned to them with a wide grin. "Well, little lady, you ready to ditch this skinny kid and get a taste of a real man?" He addressed Simone's cleavage, which, James had to admit, was appealingly displayed. Not that her clothes likely made much difference to Bob's manners. He still would have leered if she wore a nun's habit.

Simone had regained her usual social poise and sparkle after the surprise of the previous day. He had a feeling very little would shock her tonight. "Oh Mr. Taggert, you're too witty! If you see a real man anywhere around here, please let me know!" She said it with venomous sweetness. Nudging her chair closer to James, she leaned into him with an adoring look so convincing, he could almost mistake it for real. He smiled back at her, draping his arm possessively around her shoulders, then letting his fingers toy with her shoulder strap.

"Wine, my sweet?" He said it loudly enough for Bob's ears, knowing the only way he might leave Simone alone was if he believed another man "owned" her. To someone like Bob, a woman was a possession, something to be used for pleasure or status. James hated playing this game, but he would, to keep her safe. *Just for tonight.* They would not be doing this again.

"Red please, honey bear."

Honey bear?! He mouthed it back incredulously. Of all the ridiculous names...she'd pay for that.

She innocently batted her lashes as he filled her wineglass, then casually handed it to her with a kiss on the temple.

"Anything for you, *my dove.*"

She pressed her lips together, hiding a smile, before she took her first sip. Bob snorted so loudly in disgust, it sounded like fabric ripping.

Thankfully, the program was about to start. Before he could say anything else to Simone, Bob and the other key investors were called up to give a few words. The mayor began, again waxing poetic about the resort's benefit to his pocketbook, if one read between the lines.

Bob was next. James gleaned quite a few things from his short, rambling speech. He was in oil, which did not surprise him. He saw the purpose of land ownership as shaping and exploiting it for his profit, which was, likewise, entirely expected. That he had children, who must be near his and Simone's age, was also not a shock, but it made his leers at Simone even grosser.

The evening dragged on, accompanied by a complete lack of culinary surprise: decent-tasting prime rib or decent-looking stuffed chicken breast, slightly bland whipped potatoes, and passable spring vegetables.

Dick made his way to the podium with a good amount of fanfare, giving out some handshakes and back-slaps. He cleared his throat at the microphone, waiting for an assistant to unveil a large presentation board with a detailed architectural mockup.

"As some of you know, this new project for Montgomery Developing marks a new phase for the company: for our partnerships with this province and with our neighbors." He nodded to Bob. "Thanks to the successful launch of Northern Tides Resort and Spa, we will build a chain of luxury resorts across the country. Our next location will be an exclusive fly-in-only site, the perfect place to get away from it all."

Polite clapping did not quite mask a commotion in the back of the room. One of the press tables was trying to get Dick's attention.

"You will all have an opportunity for questions at a later date..."

He was cut off by a clear, high voice. "Excuse me, Mr. Montgomery, can you comment on proceeding with future development plans on unceded Anishinaabe territory against the express wishes of the surrounding communities?"

Dick looked annoyed at the interruption, trying to regain control of the room that now buzzed with low, murmured chatter.

James craned around for the speaker, his eyes finally landing on the same petite woman he'd seen earlier on the golf course with a press pass. The identity behind that heart-shaped face became crystal clear in his mind. What was her name? Dawn something.

He nudged Simone, but she waved him off, distracted by one of the servers who was offering to refill her wine.

He couldn't remember Dawn's last name, but he knew her byline was on at least half the papers in his bag. The ones he'd been meaning to talk to Simone about. There was just too much going on between them this weekend. It made his stomach churn, that familiar feeling of everything being out of control.

"I will not be answering any questions, but I can confirm that all the proper permits have been obtained, following surveys and community consultations carried out according to provincial regulations." Raising his voice, he carried on without taking a breath, as though afraid of interruption, concluding his remarks with a toast to his wife, daughter, and mother-in-law for their instrumental support.

James bristled. The whole thing stank of a coverup. And, to top it off, Dick relied on Simone just as much as he did his other family members, and yet never once thanked her. Her help was assumed but never appreciated. It was just the mud icing on a shit cake.

By the time dessert rolled around, most of the table was several drinks in, thanks to the continually-refilled cocktails and glasses of wine. He was the only abstainer. Even Simone was on her second glass, the sweet flush in her cheeks prominent, though she wasn't tipsy by any means. He supposed it was one way to make the night go faster, instead of what he endured, sitting through every long minute stone-cold sober.

But he had other ways to pass the time. His arm rested on the back of her chair whenever they weren't eating, his fingers playing with the neckline of her dress and the curls that were starting to come loose from her carefully-done hair, taking perverse pleasure in mussing her further. He scrutinized her responsive shivers, the way she'd sometimes take a gulp of wine right after. Yes, he did have a way to make the time go faster.

There was so much noise at their table, and all around the room. Simone began looking pained: she stopped reacting to his touch, instead bouncing one leg and running the chain of her clutch through her fingers. He once again rested his arm over her shoulders, this time squeezing her body into his side to help ground her. She relaxed into him, and the anxious pace of her movements slowed, to his relief. They had to get out of here soon.

Frances and Bob, on either side of the table, were going on about a rematch, which he gathered had something to do with a poker game. Each shout they volleyed back was louder than the one before.

"Where did Sam escape to, this time?" Simone muttered.

"She was gone before dessert. I should be annoyed that she always leaves you alone to deal with her family, but right now, I'm just jealous." He spoke softly into her ear, gratified by her chuckle. Impatiently, he checked his watch again.

Mabel shrieked across the table, trying to be heard above the two gamblers, "*Darlings*, why aren't you dancing?" The floor had been set up on one side of the room, a few couples already swaying there, slow-dancing to oldies.

Her shrieks cut through Bob and Frances' bickering, drawing their attention back to the table.

"I'll tell you what, I believe I'm owed a dance." Bob cut in abruptly. "I can still sweep a woman off her feet if I'm of the mind to." He turned to Simone. "Let's go, little lady."

James tightened his arm around her, but she answered coolly before he could come up with anything to say. "No thanks, Mr. Taggert. I think my grandmother is free, though. Why don't you ask her?"

"Frances?" He looked toward her grandmother, thunderclouds in his expression. "I won the girl fair and square, and I expect to be compensated." Other tables were staring

at them now, craning their necks to see what the shouting was about.

"Gran?" Simone's voice was hard as cut crystal. "What
is this man talking about?" She managed to imbue the
word 'man' with so much scorn, it practically dripped.

Frances winced but said nothing.

"Tell the girl, Frances. Tell the girl that you gambled
her to me and now she won't even give me a dance."

He reached into his wallet and pulled out a picture. It
was the headshot she'd had taken when she opened the
shelter, featuring Simone posing with one of the rescue
dogs. She was so proud of having gotten the organiza-
tion off the ground at last, she'd had copies printed for
her relatives and friends. He still had it tacked up on his
fridge.

"Oh, Bob, you're being so silly!" Frances was obviously
trying to play it off as nonsense. "It was all just a *joke*,
of course." She waved carelessly toward Simone. "I was
getting out my wallet to ante up—just a little downswing,
dearie, you know how it is—and then your picture fell
out. And for some reason, my cash had run out, and you
know the rule that whatever's on the table is fair to wager.
Of course, we had a good laugh about it. Bob took your
picture when he won that hand, and that was that. All in
good fun." She sipped her cocktail, glancing around the

table with a smile as though judging how her story had gone over.

Simone stood up, hands clenched in fury, red high on her apple cheeks. "Gran, next time you want to sell someone, wager yourself. I am *done.*"

He couldn't believe she had finally said something to her beloved grandmother. If he hadn't been so angry about the whole situation, he'd have been proud of her. With a last glare at Frances, he followed her through the tables toward the exit. They were going to finally make their escape.

"There you are!" Dick stopped them in their tracks. He had missed the whole confrontation while he was off schmoozing, which was maybe for the best. Gesturing to the couple beside him, he introduced them: "Mr. and Mrs. Han, meet my niece, Simone, and her fiancé, James. Mrs. Han expressed an interest in your stylist, Simone."

They were caught. Simone dutifully struck up a conversation with Mrs. Han about hairdressers and beauty products, while James stood nearby, trying to look purposeful. It was deflating to have all the adrenaline of rage pumping through him, with nowhere to channel it, to stand there and let it slowly seep out of him. He turned away from the women, glaring after Dick who seemed to be heading off to find someone else for Simone to talk to.

The journalist who'd spoken out earlier stepped directly into Dick's path, forcing him to address her. She was once again wearing her press badge and dressed in a brightly banded skirt with a turtle embroidered in the center. It was different than any of the formal dresses in the room but had a feeling of formality and significance. He wondered if she felt alone, standing so upright in Dick's path.

"Mr. Montgomery, I'm Dawn Bushie, and I'm here with Prairie Sky News. Can we set up a time to discuss my questions from earlier? Our readers are very interested in Montgomery's permit and consultation process."

He brushed her off. "You'll have to speak to my secretary to arrange an appointment." Turning back to Simone, he directed her toward a tall, redheaded woman lingering nearby. "Have you spoken to Mrs. Davidson? She wanted to know about your dog pound."

He stepped around Dawn, who did not look ready to give up, despite this second dismissal. She just looked thoughtful, and spoke into her phone for a minute, perhaps taking notes. Someone else wearing a press pass came up to talk to her, sympathetically, James thought.

He was interrupted by Simone's nudge in his ribs. He'd been tuned out completely. Social settings like this were just too overwhelming. Especially when everyone wanted to talk to your date.

"Hi, Mrs. Davidson! Nice to see you again. What would you like to know about our *animal shelter*?" Simone glared after her uncle, who was already hustling away. "We have several birds and a rabbit right now at Helping Paws, so it's not all raining cats and dogs." Both women laughed and settled into small talk.

James cut in after a few minutes. "Please excuse me, ladies." He tried out his best sheepish grin on Mrs. Davidson. "I promised this beautiful gal a dance, didn't I, sweet cheeks?" He took Simone by the hand, and the other woman put a hand over her heart as though witnessing the height of romance.

Simone smiled up at him, cheekily. "Lead on, baby-cakes."

The dance floor was crowded now, but he found a space and brought her close. "Sorry, it was the only thing I could think of to get you out of there. The door is too far away. We'll never make it out past your uncle."

"Uncle Dick is cramping our style. I suppose it's all worth it if it helps the family." She sighed and leaned into his chest, swaying with him in perfect time. "At least he wouldn't interrupt a dance."

"You never know, with him. He might bring Ms. Buller over here to ask you the exact shade of your lipstick."

"There is no Ms. Buller. But you do have a point."

"And how do you know there isn't? You haven't met everyone here."

"Almost. Not only that, but I've memorized most of their names and a fact or two about each. I may not study the resort brochure, but this is what I'm expected to do. They even taught a name memorization strategy in etiquette classes."

James shook his head and brought her in closer, executing a little spin to get them out of the way of an overly enthusiastic couple. "Finishing school had you covered, I guess. Too bad they didn't teach a martial art while they were at it."

"Self defense for young ladies was the closest thing we did. Remember? I practiced my chokehold break with you."

"Hell, I forgot about that." James laughed. "They really did think of everything."

He let his feet carry them, but kept his eyes open and alert. She didn't need anyone else invading her space. She'd been through enough.

Simone sighed again. "I can't believe Gran did that."

"Can't you, though?" He brushed his cheek lightly against her temple to take the sting out of his words. It was swiftly becoming one of his favorite spots to touch.

She was so sweet there. He couldn't afford to catalog his favorite spots, but he was building a ranking regardless.

"She's never been that thoughtless before."

"Hmm," he said, his tone sympathetic but noncommittal. They would have to disagree on that point, but he couldn't bear to contradict her when she was so hurt. "Hey, let's sneak out of here." He motioned to the nearby exit. "That door has to get us somewhere. We can go around the long way."

She leaned back to smile up at him. "Just like old times? Sneaking around and going on adventures?"

His heart panged, but he smiled back. "Just like old times."

ELEVEN

Simone

The stairwell was connected to nothing and nowhere. They went down a level and found a service door to a loading area. They turned back and found another door that led to the kitchens, clanging with dishes and full of clouds of steam. Neither of them felt like braving it. They went up yet another level, which led to a blank corridor that also seemed to be for service.

"I don't like the looks of this one," James said doubt-fully. He was too close behind, probably because she had slowed down significantly. Her feet were starting to hurt, and traipsing up and down stairs had left her winded, though she didn't like to admit it to him, the distance runner. Her lungs usually held up just fine, but his were on another level. She tried to gasp for air quietly enough that he couldn't hear her.

"It'll be fine." She kept her answer short to preserve her breath. She wasn't about to do another flight of stairs in heels.

They wandered down the hallway, finding store-rooms of different sizes holding cleaning carts and paper products. They were halfway down the corridor when a door at the other end of the hall opened. Two people exited and walked toward them, talking to each other.

"Quick! In here," she hissed, opening the nearest door. With the dim light from the hall, she could see a room crammed full of large mechanical floor sweepers and polishers.

James reluctantly followed before she pulled the door closed behind him.

"You're being ridiculous. There's no reason to hide. We can just ask them where to go." He sounded long-suffering. Even in the dark, you could practically hear the eye roll.

"No, no, no. I'm supposed to be serious and represent the company. I can't skulk around." She whispered it furiously. Of course, he refused to cooperate.

He sighed deeply, his breath moving her hair. The room was so crowded, there was barely any floor space left to stand in. "And yet, here you are, skulking. Just walk normally out into the hall and tell them you got lost. Lay on the charm."

"Excuse me," she hissed. "*We* got lost."

The hotel employees were still nearby. Their voices sounded close and stationary. Hopefully, they didn't plan to use one of the machines in this room. That would be embarrassing. James was right, as usual. She should just walk out of here, lay the charm on thick, and ask for directions.

It was just that she was charmed out for the evening. She couldn't take any more strangers, any more maneuvering, any more polite smiles. Even though it was completely illogical, and she'd be happier in their hotel room watching the tub fill with steaming hot water, she was incapable of doing anything but standing here in the cool dark with James until they were alone again.

"Hey." He lifted her chin, trying to see her face in the faint light from the small window in the door. He sounded concerned. "You okay?"

Tears gathered in the corners of her eyes and prickled at her nose. She was nowhere in the vicinity of okay. And James was the only one in this place, maybe the only person in the whole world, who cared. She sniffled. A small sound, but it was loud in that quiet space.

"Hey," he said again, but this time his voice aimed to soothe and comfort. His arms went around her; she let herself fall into them, let them anchor her again as they had all day.

They stood there for a time, the dark room filled with nothing but their breathing and the murmur of voices from the hall. This was their blissful little secret. She laid her head on his shoulder and brushed her nose against his neck, taking the liberty of that small nuzzle, the musk notes from his shaving cream strong and heady. It was going to be sad to go back to not touching him at all.

It was her turn to sigh, with regret, not irritation. He shivered as her breath blew across his throat, his arms tightening around her briefly before relaxing again. Now, this was interesting. She'd had a response to him earlier that had been almost mortifying in its intensity. A few minutes more and she might have begged him to pin her down and have his way with her. She still felt the echoes of his lips on her neck. She had a feeling they might linger forever.

Perhaps it was time for a little turnaround: he'd done all this to her, and it hardly seemed fair. The idea of reducing him to begging for her was intoxicating. Her lips curved against his shoulder, but she hesitated. If he rejected her, she didn't know how she could handle it. If he went cold; if he told her she was being ridiculous yet again, her ego might never recover. Plausible deniability was what she wanted. She'd have to take it slow.

She stretched in his arms, snuggling closer, pressing her breasts into his chest. The little sound he made in his throat was a promising start. Backing a half-step away was less promising, but, on the other hand, now he was up against the door, which was kind of hot.

He rubbed his hands briskly up and down her arms. "Gonna be okay?" he whispered, as though he was trying to put them back in friend territory. It would have been more effective if he hadn't brushed against the sides of her breasts with his thumbs, then made another half-strangled sound.

She grabbed the lapels of his suit, holding them firmly and stepping close to trap him against the door. His swallow was audible, and if he could have seen the triumphant look on her face, he might have run. He wanted her, she was sure of it. But could she get him to admit it?

"I've been thinking," she said, in her most casual tone, speaking softly to avoid anyone hearing from the hallway. "And, well, you got to kiss me earlier, and you put your hands on me. I've been wondering if maybe we should even the score."

"Even the score." He repeated it as though he didn't understand the words.

Sometimes high heels were worth the trouble, because her mouth was so conveniently close to his. A light brush over his lips served to clarify her meaning.

"Simone." He sounded like he was summoning strength. "You want to kiss me?"

Well, when he put it that way, no. What she wanted was for him to melt into a puddle like she had for him. She wanted to balance the scales of power and lust, but they seemed to have tipped exclusively in his direction. "Only if you ask me nicely. My mouth is a rare commodity."

"That's not what Lucas said in high school."

She gasped. Then drew away, or tried to. Why was he ruining this? His hands gripped her upper arms again, keeping her against him.

"So," he drawled, his voice a contrast to his tensed fingers. Cocky. Infuriating. "You want to put your mouth and hands all over me, and you want me to beg you for it." She tried to protest, but there was nowhere to go in that small patch of clear floor, and he still held her firm. He continued as if she hadn't said anything. "Do you have any parameters?"

"What do you mean?" She spat it out stiffly.

"Parameters, Larson," He asked, his tone carelessly lazy. This was a whole new side of James, an alternate dimension. "Anywhere you won't touch me?"

"No." She squinted at his face, trying to see his expression. But it was so dark, and the light was behind him. "I'll touch you anywhere you want me to." It was too revealing, but the simple truth.

One of his hands trailed down her arm till he was holding her fingers in his. "How about here?" He guided her touch to the front of his dress pants, where she discovered he was hard and thick under her palm. She clenched around his erection convulsively, both of them panting now.

"This is what you want?" she breathed. Steam could have been pouring from between her lips. She had his cock in her hand; he had been hard, wanting her. She might boil away on the spot.

"No," he panted. His hand, wrapped around her wrist, was holding her there, or holding her still; she couldn't tell which. "It's what *you* want. I want..." He paused, a tremor running through him. "Just kiss me. Please."

That was good enough for her, though she had lost track of who the scales were tipping toward now. She kept her hand right where it was, tracing the outline of him under his zipper, and reached up to take his mouth with hers. A flick of her tongue, a scrape of her teeth, and he was opening for her, letting her in past all his defenses, a heady pleasure. His hands came up to cradle her face, leaving hers free to work at his belt buckle.

She kissed along his jaw and undid the button, going slow, giving him time to rethink, to pause if he needed to. As she pulled down his zipper, she returned to his mouth, kissing him hard enough to press the back of his head flush against the door's firm surface, the perfect counter-pressure to her onslaught.

His erection came free: it was a pleasure to run her hands all over it, already a little slippery at the head, working the moisture up and down his satiny smooth shaft until he was whimpering into her mouth and thrusting into her hands. He had gone from drawling detachment to on the brink so fast, she could still feel the whiplash.

She had wanted to take him apart, but this was more like tearing him to pieces. His hands clamped around her head, feasting at her mouth. Every frantic move-ment of his hips made her writhe helplessly along with him. She tried to soothe him, tried to slow him down and get him to make it last. They had time. But he pistoned faster into her grip. She loosened her fingers around him and reached one hand down to his balls, trying to give him something different so he could slow down.

It backfired dramatically. He buried his face in her neck and came loudly, bucking against her with his arms crushed around her.

She stood, stunned, her fingers coated in semen, a large wet spot spreading on her dress, with James leaning on her heavily, breathing like he'd run a marathon. What was she supposed to do now? The etiquette classes hadn't covered this one. Making your friend since forever blow all over you in a matter of moments wasn't in the rule book.

She pressed a brief kiss to his cheek, letting go of his rapidly softening cock, stepping back as far as possible without falling over the equipment. The hallway outside was quiet and probably had been for a while. Her hands, she wiped on her dress. It was already wet.

Fumbling for the latch, she opened the door a crack. It was all clear. The sound of his zipper pulling closed was loud in the previous silence, making her jump.

"Let's go get cleaned up. I want to get out of these shoes and into a hot bath." She kept it light and casual, wanting to give him the opportunity to brush off what'd happened. Was it just her, or had that been extra intense?

"I. Uh. Yeah." He coughed, awkwardly. "Let's go."

Back in their room, in the bathroom with the bath fill-ing, she mused on how to bring this up with him. The walk back to their room, in a soaked dress that stuck to her skin and shoes that pinched her toes, had been blessedly short. But right now, she wished she'd had more time to think. He'd trailed after her like a silent shadow, not even speaking when she took a wrong turn and doubled back. What was going through his head?

Testing the water temperature, she added a bath bomb that she'd brought along. Baths were no place for austerity. Perched on the toilet lid, she watched it swirl and fizz, sending pink streamers through the water and filling the air with roses. It should have been meditative, but she couldn't find any calm.

Once it was filled to her satisfaction, she exited the bathroom to collect her toiletry bag, having taken off her sticky dress and put on her robe. Taking her earlier seat in front of the mirror, she removed her bobby pins, tying up her curls in a loose topknot.

"Last chance to use the bathroom before I sink be-neath the waves forever." She smiled in his direction, but couldn't quite meet his eyes. He still had smears of lipstick around his mouth, which was unspeakably hot. He looked rumpled, debauched, and defiled, his curly hair frizzed from running through it with his hands, his shirt half untucked and his tie loosened.

He cleared his throat. "Okay, let me get a couple of things." He scuttled sideways into the bathroom. She didn't think he even looked at her.

Once she was done fussing with her hair, she glanced his way again. He was seated on the couch, head in his hands, the picture of frustration and misery. She wanted to stand between his knees, tilting his head toward hers, looking into his eyes until she broke through. Until he told her what she needed to hear. But she couldn't. She didn't know if she'd be welcome. Maybe what they both needed was space.

TWELVE

James

He'd lost his mind. There was no other explanation for it. She'd put her hands on him...no, *he'd* put them there. And then he'd been towed under by a riptide that hadn't let him surface until he'd come all over her, gasping for air. He groaned and tugged at his hair again. What was wrong with him?

She was acting so normal now, like she did this kind of thing every day. Maybe for her it was no big deal, but to him, it was a sea change. It was his fault. Touching her all day long, kissing her yesterday, had been slowly but surely drugging him. He was high off her skin and her proximity, and off the idea that he could belong to her. All of that had made him completely lose his sense of reason or normalcy until he sincerely thought it had been okay to *take her hand and put it on his dick*. Fuck.

But it was his fault. He'd known that touching her could lead him down this road, the same way he knew a few sips of liquor could lead him down a darker path. That was why he abstained. He just couldn't quite make himself understand that abstaining from her was for the best. He needed a clean break, to go cold turkey. The problem was that she always felt like home, and he couldn't bear to rip himself away from her.

The splashes and drips from the bath were driving him crazy. Those damned too-thin hotel doors. He'd just decided to drown out the sounds with the TV when something faintly buzzed, its noise unfamiliar. He checked his phone. No reception still. Hunting through the room for its source, he found her phone tossed in a corner of her tote bag. Silent. But the buzzing continued. And was that a *moan*?

No force in the world could have kept him from that bathroom door. His hand grasped the handle before he could stop himself. *Wait.* What the hell was he doing? He laid his forehead on the panel in frustration. He shouldn't be here. But the rippling sounds, the faint buzzing, the low whimpers, they could only mean one thing. And he wondered if what she was doing by herself, alone, was all she wanted.

"Everything okay in there?"

She gasped. The buzzing stopped.

"Fine, thank you." Her voice was so much higher than usual, it was almost squeaky. He could almost picture her blush.

"Are you sure there's nothing I can help you with?" *Please, let me help.* He lightly banged his forehead against the jamb. If this kept on, he was going to go straight to the gym to do wind sprints until he collapsed. His hand still clenched the doorknob; as he waited for her to answer, he slowly uncurled his fingers. She wasn't going to say anything, and he should just go now.

"If you really want to help, I'm trying to get off right now." She said it crisply, in her normal register. Simone had never been much for shame. "Some of us got worked up and didn't get to finish earlier."

"Are you sure you're okay if I join you?" His hand was back on the knob, already turning.

"Yes." Again, clear and calm. She was a marvel. He turned the knob the last fraction, until the door finally opened.

The tub was deep, which he suspected would not be the case in a less fancy hotel bathroom. She reclined in opaque pink water that barely covered the tops of her breasts, her knees peeking above the water. Her hair was piled loosely on the top of her head with a scrunchie wrapped around it, escaped curls kissing her rounded bare shoulders. Her face was rosy pink and free of makeup. She was all softness, curves, and heat.

The bathroom was so filled with steam, it was like stepping into another world, intimate and misty. He was glad he still had his contacts in. His glasses would have fogged immediately, and he couldn't miss a moment of this.

She raised one hand, water flowing in a little stream down her arm. It held a small pink toy shaped vaguely like one of her lipstick tubes.

"Is that what I think it is?" He stood beside the bath, catching tantalizing glimpses of her body through the water as she moved. He ached to put his hands all over her, but this time, he was determined not to lose his mind. He was going to focus. He was going to please her until she was the one who lost all reason.

"Depends on whether or not you think it's a vibrator." She smirked. How she could sound so cool when she was glistening with steam, flushing pink down to her freckled shoulders, was a mystery.

He couldn't smirk back or take this lightly. He had too much of her to take in. Sitting down on the closed toilet, he began rolling up his shirtsleeves. He didn't care if he got thoroughly soaked; if she let him, he was getting his hands in that tub.

"Want to show me how you use it?" He couldn't help that his voice rasped. Or that his eyes were probably burning holes into her. He kept his hands busy cuffing his shirt, his gaze on her.

She flushed an even deeper shade, but flicked it on. The buzz echoed in the tiled room.

"Are you planning to at least come over here and kiss me?"

"In a minute."

She closed her eyes briefly, as if summoning strength, then slid her toy under the water. Her breasts bobbed and flashed him with glimpses of her peaked nipples. He leaned forward, clasping his hands to keep them occupied, resting his elbows on his knees. He would be patient if it killed him.

He couldn't see most of her body, or what she was doing under the water, but he didn't need to. Her head tipped back, and she crossed her arm over the center of her body, plumping one breast higher, exposing even more of her perfect nipple. She was lit up with pleasure, making him ache to crawl into her softness and never leave. Flexing her arm, she moved her hand under the water and sighed. The buzzing was burrowing into his mind. He didn't think he'd ever forget that sound or her expression.

Without conscious thought, he was on his knees beside the tub. She opened her eyes to look him over, lingering on his mouth and open shirt collar, surveying him down to his rolled-up shirtsleeves before she once again met his stare. He probably looked as raw and undone as he felt, but she didn't seem to mind.

"Planning on kissing me any time soon?" The hand that wasn't underwater, working, came to rest on his chest. Wet heat instantly dampened his shirt, and he shivered.

"Where can I touch you?"

She smiled. "You can touch me anywhere you want to."

His fingers dipped into the water, testing. As he suspected, it was near scalding. No wonder she was so pink. She was steaming herself like a lobster.

The heat of the water faded as he arrived at the peak of her breasts. He brushed against them, flicking his eyes to hers as she sharply inhaled. She watched his hands on her body with utter absorption. The buzzing stopped as he brushed her nipples again, enjoying the way her breasts floated and bobbed in the water. Gathering one in his palm just to feel its weight, he leaned over the tub to find her mouth. They made out while he kneaded her breast under his hand, its slippery smoothness and firm, textured nipple a delight to the touch.

All his senses were overwhelmed by her again. Kissing her for the third time was already like coming home, gentler and more sensual than their frenzied kisses in that dark room.

He broke away. "I need to say, I've never done this before."

Her hand on the side of his face was gentle. "This is new territory for both of us. If you want to stop, I get it."

"I don't think you understand." He rolled a nipple between his fingers, hoping the pressure wasn't too hard, watching her closely to see if she liked it. She shuddered and tilted her head to the side, exposing her throat to him. Nibbling there seemed like a fantastic idea. He was going to have to climb into the bath to get all the access to her he wanted.

With effort, he got back on track, keeping one hand on her breast and one twined in her hair. He cleared his throat. "What I mean is, I've never done any of this before. Touched another person, or had someone, uh, touch me like that." Shit, he was getting flustered. He needed her to understand. "Simone, I'm a virgin."

She leaned into his hand and, with a fist in his shirt, tried to pull his head down to her again. "Virginity is a construct."

"Okay. That's fine. It doesn't change the fact that I've never done this before. You're going to need to show me what you like. And, uh, I might get a little too excited. Again."

Her smile was so seductive, he was at her lips before he realized he'd moved. Her mouth under his was so sweet, full and plush and biteable. All of her was delicious. They kissed until he was breathless and then beyond, until he forgot that breathing was required, until his lungs were full of her. She sucked his tongue into her mouth, a move that had made him frantic earlier, and was no less potent now. It was a promise, he now realized, of what her mouth could do to him. If he'd thought her hands were deadly, this was much more dangerous.

Taking his hand in hers, she guided it under the water and down her body, over her soft rolls, then lower.

"Go do some exploring and see what you find," she broke free long enough to say. "I'll be here if you need me." Drawing him back into her kiss, she ran her tongue over his teeth. Her lips curved under his, while his hand discovered new horizons.

It was hard to focus with her mouth moving so hungrily against his, when he wanted to home in on her curls and folds, finding out how she liked to be touched. She'd figured him out almost immediately, after all. He trailed his fingers up and down, trying to please her. But when he tried to dip a finger inside her, she stopped him with a hand on his wrist.

"I don't want dirty bathwater shoved up there. You can do that later." Well, that thought held promise. Not that they could actually do anything penetrative. He had never even bought condoms before. But her hands had been more than enough for him, and maybe his hands could give her a similar pleasure.

She guided him to place his finger on what he could only assume was her clit, then showed him how to circle it in a little half-moon pattern, humming in approval as he caught on. Her hand fell away. "And then occasionally go right over the top of it." She instructed. He complied. "Yes, like *that*, do that."

It was an awkward angle, straining his wrist, but he wouldn't have stopped even if it was painful. She was glorious like this. Her chest heaving, hips lifting, head twisting, begging him not to stop. Both of her hands gripped his arm, instinctively trying to hold him in place, water rippling and sloshing over the sides as she anchored herself in the deep tub. He was rapidly getting as wet as her, his shirt glued to his arms and torso.

"Kiss me, James," she breathed, sounding frantic. "I need more."

His other hand found its way back into her hair as he kissed her deeply, swallowing her moans. Pressing her into the towel she'd rolled up as a headrest, he tried to moor her so that she could let herself go. He swirled his finger faster, his touch a little firmer. He was rewarded when she broke, gloriously, tensing around his hand and trapping it between her full thighs, writhing, splashing. With a final cry, she subsided, loose-limbed and wrung out, panting hard.

Her thighs parted enough for him to leave the marvelous new spot he'd found. He didn't want to go, but he made himself sit back on his heels and give her some space. But he couldn't resist playing with her hair, pulling on a long curl and letting it spring back.

She batted his hand away. "Quit that. You're going to fuzz my curls."

He grinned back. "So, how was that?"

"Not too bad for a first-timer." She looked amused. "I'll give you a full report after I drain the bath and rinse off." She paused. "Alone."

That was as direct a dismissal as he'd ever had. As much as he wanted to plead with her to let him stay, they were even now. An orgasm for an orgasm, and plenty of fodder for his imagination later. He couldn't ask much more than that.

He got up, slowly and reluctantly, putting down two towels to help with all the flooding. He was wetter than he'd realized. Snagging another towel, he went to dry himself off in the other room. They'd need to call room service to get more at this rate.

"James," she called. He paused with a hand on the door. "Um, can you please take a picture of yourself right now and send it to me?"

He glanced at the mirror. His white shirt had gone see-through, clinging to him like a second skin. Even his pants were molded to his body, outlining the erection he'd gotten while pleasing her. She liked what she saw? It made him giddy. Their eyes connected in the mirror. She had been staring at him with open hunger, her glance sweeping up and down his body.

He set his palms on the bathroom counter and leaned forward, still holding her stare in the mirror. It was better than turning to look at her directly. The foggy mirror helped lessen the impact of her by a few crucial degrees. His fingers tensed with the effort of keeping himself there, but he kept his voice casual. "If I send you a picture, will you look at it when you take out your vibrator later? I just want to know exactly what use it'll be put to."

"Well, I do find this look on you extremely...inspirational."

"Then I'll send it to you on one condition." He lifted a finger admonishingly. "That you text me any time you use it as *inspiration*." He left before he could find an excuse to put his hands on her.

THIRTEEN
Simone

They had made such a huge mess. She was grateful for downtime under the shower spray, its water cooler than usual. Between the hot bath and James' incendiary fingers, she was dangerously overheated.

She fought a small war with herself over what to do about James as she finished rinsing off. After cleaning up the sopping towels, now tinged pink from her bath bomb, she tried to dry herself with one of the tiny hand cloths still left. They had never done anything like this. For the sake of their friendship, she should walk out there pretending it hadn't happened; she should stuff it in a vault and throw away the key. But the problem was, she didn't want to. She wanted to take him by his bony shoulders and teach him exactly what she liked.

He would be such an attentive student. The memory of his intense concentration made her hot all over again, and she lost the thread of her internal argument.

What she should do and what she was going to do were two entirely different things.

But first, they should talk.

She belted her short satin robe around the sexy underwear she'd shimmied into. Maybe she was being scandalous, but the man had made her come in the bath. He could handle seeing a little skin, and her trusty balconette bra would be his reward for a job well done.

She eyed herself in the still-foggy mirror. Balconettes in her size were a feat of engineering as impressive as the Eiffel Tower. It fit perfectly, the gore snugged up against her breastbone, its demi-cups barely covering her nipples and exposing two temptingly plumped mounds. Considering both the bra and her matching pink lace panty were see-through, if he didn't collapse begging at her feet, there was no hope for him. Her obsession with expensive underwear was about to be put to excellent use.

She fluffed her hair, letting it fall around her shoulders. Primping for James should have felt strange, but anticipation buoyed her. He could play with her hair as much as he wanted, as long as he was touching her, and as long as she was the center of all his considerable attention.

One last glance in the mirror, one last steadying breath, a quick rummage through her toiletry bag, and she was ready to knock him dead. She'd regained her equilibrium, and she wasn't going to let him throw her off again.

He'd taken out his contacts and put his glasses back on. He'd also changed into a tee and jeans, which struck her as odd compared to her outfit choice. Their vibes were decidedly different. Either he trusted in the seductive power of denim (fair), or he was putting on armor and hoping it would keep her out. She'd have to feel him out carefully on that one.

Unfortunately, he had immediately spotted the condom foil glinting between her fingers, judging by the way the color left his face. Subtlety had flown out the window.

"Is that what I think it is?" he rasped.

"It depends on whether you think it's a condom." They were back in a conversational echo that made her laugh, inappropriately. It was a nervous reaction she'd never been able to restrain.

He lifted his glasses and pinched the bridge of his nose, which made her want to laugh harder, but she swallowed it down at the last second. If he knew how sexy he was at that moment, she'd never hear the end of it.

"Are you telling me"—he put his glasses back on and glared at her through them—"that you *planned* for this?" Even the glare was hot. There was something wrong with her.

"No, no, absolutely not." She laughed again, helplessly, reaching out to him entreatingly before she realized that the condom between her fingers made it look as though she was offering it to him. "I found it at the bottom of my travel kit. I only have one, so if it's too old and it breaks, that's all we've got. But we don't have to do anything. I just was wondering, if you've never done it before, if you wanted to."

"So, this is a pity fuck?" He managed to imbue the words with so much scorn, it was difficult to hear the vulnerability behind them. Unless you knew him.

"I think you know that's not what this is. You know me better than that."

"Sorry." He turned from her, shoving a hand in his hair again. "I just don't know what this all means for us. I've lost track of why we're doing this."

That stung, but she tried not to show it. "It doesn't have to mean anything deep. But if you want to pop that cherry, I'm willing to help."

He mouthed 'pop that cherry' disbelievingly back at her, shaking his head. At least he was looking at her again. "I thought you said virginity was a construct."

"I was trying to lighten the mood."

"It's not working."

"Fine. You don't want to do this. I get it." She was starting to get frustrated. "Let's put a movie on and pretend it never happened. I'll put this away." She slipped the condom into the pocket of her robe, where she should have had it the entire time.

It was beneath her to plop down on the couch and pick up the remote in a huff, but it was better than revealing the wound he'd opened. Was there anything worse than putting yourself out there, hopeful and shiny-eyed, and being rejected? The TV menu scrolled past as she stared at it determinedly, not absorbing a single bit of information. She was too aware of him. James threw up his hands in frustration, moving to the other end of the couch. Out of the corner of her eye, she could see him turned toward her, waiting for her to stop being childish. He'd have a long wait.

James cleared his throat. "This might not be a big deal to you, but it is to me. You're the first person I've ever done anything like this with because I'm just not interested in anyone else that way."

She stopped scrolling to look at him. He looked deeply uncomfortable, but earnest.

"What do you mean?"

"I don't know how to explain it. I tried dating a bit, especially in college, or at parties where everyone else was pairing off, tried to fool around like everyone else. But it just made me uncomfortable, and I would leave." He laughed bitterly. "Maybe I'm just not wired the same way as everyone else. I can't do hookups. You're the first person I've actually wanted to do more than kiss."

She should make some sort of response, not just stare at him blankly. Her usual facility with words was gone, but she had to say something before he shut down completely. "I'm glad you're comfortable with me. And I'm glad you told me."

He smiled, but it looked like a wince. He turned away and the silence stretched.

The problem was, this confession was an awful lot of pressure. She'd planned to saunter out in her sexy underwear, smirk, banter a bit, and watch him fall at her feet. They'd let desire sweep them along until bad decisions could be dismissed as impulsive moments not worth a second thought. Being the only one he wanted? Something else entirely.

But he deserved an equally vulnerable response. "It's not my first time." Obviously. He had known most of her boyfriends and heard about some of her hookups. "But that doesn't mean it's not a big deal. You're important to me, and I don't want to mess up anything with you." She laughed again, knowing it wasn't the right reaction, but unable to repress her nerves. He was still quiet. "Waltzing out with a condom was a little presumptive of me. That orgasm must have affected me more than I thought. It'll be okay. We'll put all this behind us when we check out and go back to normal."

She was babbling now. Pressing her lips closed, she turned back to the TV menu. Surely there had to be something that would flip the mood. She'd been hoping that their back-to-normal could wait another day, maybe two, before they dealt with all the ramifications.

Not that it changed what had happened between them, but since they'd arrived, it was as though they'd been playing pretend. So far, she liked this imaginary world. The real one sucked by comparison.

Shifting in her seat, she opened her robe a little further at the neckline, uncovering most of her pink lace bra. She didn't know if she could tempt him to stay in the land of pretend with her, but she sure wanted to try.

"Are you doing that on purpose?" His voice was low, intense.

"What if I am?" She didn't look at him, but heard him moving along the couch, stalking toward her.

"Do you want me, Simone?" He was close now, staring down at her, his jeans rubbing against her bare knee, his arm wrapped around the back of the couch behind her, his eyes moving from her mouth to bare shoulder to cleavage and back again.

He played with the lapel of her robe, running his fingers up and down the smooth satin, brushing against her chest with each pass. With only that little, she was ready to spontaneously combust. He didn't do anything else as he waited for her answer. She stretched up toward him, trying to reach his mouth, but he dodged, placing his hand in her hair to cradle her head. His eyes were serious.

"Answer the question, Simone."

She shivered. "Yes," she said helplessly.

His mouth came down on hers in the sweetest reward; with a contented sigh, as though he were settling in for the long haul. Her neck craned sideways and back as his hand tangled in her hair, yet she was perfectly willing to be uncomfortable, so long as the kiss continued. In her experience, sometimes the anticipation of a kiss was better than the reality. But the way his lips moved on hers showed her that some experiences were better than dreams of them could ever be.

She shouldn't have been surprised at his quiet confidence, even while doing something new to him. That was so James. Once he decided, he was all in.

Shifting, she turned into him, easing the angle of her neck and throwing one leg over his lap to encourage his touch.

He broke away, leaning his forehead into hers for one sweet moment before tilting back. His glasses were fogged around the edges, and, once again, she couldn't help her delighted chuckle, this time not nervous or out of place. He was adorable. She wanted to do this forever.

The smile he returned was brief, fading into slack-jawed lust. She looked down at her breasts, nearly spilled out of her demi-cups, then back to his face.

"You can touch them if you'd like," she said, in her throatiest, most seductive voice. If he didn't start soon, he was going to hear about it.

His hand landed on her thigh instead, stroking upwards over the lace of her underwear, playing with its banded edge, and up higher still, sweeping along her body to the underside of one bra cup. He tugged at it, gently enough that she didn't have to scold him about bra prices, releasing her nipple completely from its lace cage.

He dipped his head down, slowly, eying her along the way, giving her time to pull back. She arched up into his mouth, closing the gap as much as she could, desperate for him. The wet heat of his mouth was perfect. Holding onto his head, she tried to keep him there as long as possible.

He looked up, releasing her nipple and ignoring her protests. "We've fooled around in a closet and in the bathroom. What do you think about trying the bed this time?"

She was gratified that he sounded a little unsteady, but he was still fairly calm. Maybe he was making up for losing it completely earlier. She wouldn't mind a halfway point between the two.

"You can have me anywhere," she said quietly.

Walking over to the bed, she let her robe slip off her shoulders in a satiny puddle, making sure to take the condom out of her pocket and leave it on the nightstand for later. She turned, one breast still spilling out of her bra, and posed for him, a hand on one hip, letting him take her in.

He cleared his throat. "I like your—outfit."

"Thanks. I like yours," she laughed back.

He looked down at his tee and jeans a little sheepishly.

She laughed again. "I've taken off my robe. Maybe you could take off your shirt? Just for fairness' sake. You understand."

He grinned at her, shy and adorable. And lifted his shirt over his head in one smooth sweep. Nothing she hadn't seen before, but certainly different when she would soon have the chance to get her hands on all that skin, feel his light dusting of hair against her palms, watch his lean, spare muscles tense and dance under her touch. He placed his hand on the top button of his jeans, pausing to look at her. Apparently, they were taking turns.

She reached for her bra hooks and smirked. "Now, do the rest."

He took a bracing breath, unbuttoned, then pushed down his jeans and underwear at the same time, shocking her. She had expected a slow tease. But he never did quite what she expected.

He was all sharp angles. But to her, he was beautiful.

She slowly shimmied out of her lace underwear, while James stared, open-mouthed. He was so busy taking in her weighty breasts and soft belly, her dimpled and rounded thighs, that he nearly tripped on his jeans as he moved toward her while trying to look everywhere at once. She couldn't even laugh because her throat was caught on the tenderness of this moment, seeing each other this way for the first time, looking before they touched.

Once her underwear was on the floor, she held out her hand in invitation. He took it and kissed it, slowly, lingering on her knuckles and gently nipping the side of one finger, smiling when she shivered.

"I have a condom waiting," she whispered, already desperately impatient.

"I want to touch you first." He blushed, adorably. "In case it's over too soon again."

Maybe it was too much to expect a first-timer to learn to delay, to slow down or pull out when he was close, and back away from the edge. They could play with that another time. The outside world encroached with that thought. She pushed it away, trying to stay in the present.

At her eager nod, he helped her lie back on the bed, skimming his hands over her body, hesitantly at first, then more certain. His hands and mouth on her were pure pleasure. So thorough, so awestruck. He kissed his way down, encouraged by her sighs to linger on the spots she liked best, until she was pointedly guiding him down to her clit.

He skipped it, kissing along her thighs to her knees, raising her foot to nibble at her instep and ankle. Seeing him kneeling in front of her, naked and unselfconscious, was almost too much to bear. She tried to snap a mental picture, to cement it in her mind forever, no matter what happened later. For this one perfect moment, he was worshiping at her feet, even though she was the supplicant, begging him for more.

Finally, he kissed his way higher, settling between her thighs, spreading her open for him to slowly explore. She suffered through a multitude of tentative touches and brushes that had her ready to scream in frustration. When he finally eased a finger inside, she almost sobbed in relief. Maybe she did sob in actuality. She certainly asked for more. A second finger followed: he obeyed her directions until he found a spot that had her grinding onto his hand.

Finally, she put her own hand on her clit, since he seemed too fascinated by his fingers sliding inside her to remember it.

For a minute, he watched her curiously, his expression fixed. "I'll do it," he said gruffly, moving her hand away.

Leaning down, he put his mouth right on her. His was not the most skilled tongue, but she rode his mouth and his hand with enthusiasm, scrunching the blankets in her fists and urging him on until all the tension in her broke and cleared, flinging her into blissful release. She flopped back, head buzzing, her body somehow light and heavy at the same time.

He laid down alongside her, playing with her hair and looking deeply, smugly satisfied. Maybe a little too proud of himself.

She fumbled for the condom on the side table with fingers that were still clumsy and limbs that felt uncoordinated. Smiling, she ripped open the package and leaned over to him. He had raised himself on one elbow, watching her like a hawk, cock jutting straight out in front of him.

"Roll over, dummy." She shooed at him, directing him to fall onto his back to give her access.

He snorted. "I think I like 'Babycakes' better."

But he rolled over and rested his arms behind his head. If he'd crossed his leg at the ankle and had trunks on, he could have been lounging on a beach chair.

She gripped his erection in one hand, enjoying the hiss of his breath and the minuscule lift of his hips. He was not quite as relaxed as he looked. "How are you so calm about this?"

He stared at her intently. "Because it feels like a dream, Simone. It feels like a dream I'll wake up from at the exact wrong moment." He sounded so somber.

The mood had shifted into something she wasn't prepared for, and tears pricked her eyes. Blinking them away, she rolled the condom over him with reverence. She wished this was real. She prayed it wouldn't end.

Rising, she sat astride him. He looked extremely pleased to be under her. Who said big girls couldn't ride? She slid down onto his cock slowly, carefully, teasingly, enjoying how his shoulders corded and his teeth gritted.

"It's so hot," he ground out. No hands behind his head now. No, his fingers were biting into her thighs; they sunk into her as she sunk onto him. Being filled with him was a joy that brought hot tears up to the surface again. She so rarely cried. But she was raw today.

"Fuck," he panted, after she was finally seated fully, perfectly balanced on his hips. "I'm—" Groaning, he threw his head back and gritted his teeth. He looked like he was in pain. "I'm not going to last."

The catalog of groans had a brand-new entry. It was filed under 'sex tortured': the one where his eyes glazed and he was so close to the edge he looked barely conscious.

She leaned forward, resting her weight on one hand while smoothing the other over his shoulder and down his arm reassuringly. "It's okay, just relax. I'll wait until you're ready."

Slowly, gradually, some of the tension left him. The tendons in his chest stood out less, and his hands relaxed on her thighs. She squeezed around his erection to test him. He huffed a breath, but still seemed in control.

She leaned over him, close to his mouth. "Ready for more?"

FOURTEEN

James

It was impossible to be ready for her, but he found himself nodding anyway.

There was too much to take in. The feeling of her slow, rolling pace over him, heat and unbearably good friction. The give of her hips between his hands, the sound of her soft sighs. It was sensory overload. He wanted to squeeze his eyes shut and focus on sorting through the sensations, desperate to remember everything. But he couldn't look away from her. Glistening skin, her rosy glow, the intensity in her eyes, her glorious body arrayed above him. It was a rare and perfect sight.

For a change, she was the quiet, watchful one, while he kept opening his mouth and letting all his thoughts fall out.

"So pretty." He realized he was allowed to touch the breasts softly bouncing in front of him and gathered them in his palms. "So perfect." He strained upward to bury his face between them, then fell back again, overwhelmed.

She paused. It took a moment for the ringing in his ears to clear enough to hear himself saying, "Wait." He gasped it desperately, holding her hips down. Once again, he was on the edge.

It wasn't just that he wanted to last for her sake. It was for his own, too. He couldn't bear for this to end. He'd take any amount of suffering just to make this last.

As her hands smoothed over his chest, careful and soothing, he eased back from the brink. She seemed to know exactly when he was ready for her to move again.

Being at the center of her attention was intoxicating. He had never felt so seen, so cared for. For the second time that day, he could just lie back and receive. He should have felt selfish, but he mostly felt grateful.

"Simone. Do that again." Another slow roll of her hips with a little bounce at the end that shoved him in so deeply, he saw stars. Her secret smile as she watched him react made him want to kiss her. That perfect, sassy mouth.

"Baby." He lost his train of thought when she rose further, then slid all the way down his dick. So deep, so good. For a second, he couldn't tell if he was already coming.

"Yes?" she cooed.

Too smug. This couldn't go unanswered. Squeezing her hips hard, he thrust upward while grinding her against himself, satisfied when she gasped and clung to him. He loved the soft bite of her nails and the way her head fell back in wordless response. Pleasing her was his new favorite activity.

"I want you to finish again," he whispered. *Shit*. This wasn't the time to get shy. Not when they both were sweaty and panting and he was buried balls-deep inside her. "I want you to come all over my cock," he ground out. "How can I make you come?" It was nearly a plea.

"Oh god," she moaned. "Don't stop." She leaned forward, changing the angle of his thrusts.

He couldn't resist reaching for two handfuls of her delicious ass, squeezing it as he pumped into her. With her breasts around his face and legs astride his hips, she surrounded him everywhere for a few perfect heartbeats. He'd never been so happy in his entire life.

"James."

He fell back enough to look up at her, running his hands along her legs, feeling them tremble. Those beautiful thighs squeezing around his hips. He would kiss them later. She was asking him something, but he'd been too distracted to hear.

"Sorry, what?"

She let out a frustrated sound. "Will you keep talking, like you did before? I liked that." She ground her hips to meet his body and whimpered again.

She was slowly killing him, and she wanted him to speak? He couldn't tell if she was close or not. He had no idea if he could wait for her. He didn't know which angle or thrust she liked best, or how to get her off. But he would try his best.

Her breasts were calling to him again. He gently rolled a nipple between his fingers. She might have gasped, but it was hard to hear over the rushing blood in his ears. His world narrowed to the rhythm of his hips pushing against her and the feel of her nipples in his palms. Words began pouring out of him, everything he'd been holding off on saying for so long.

"God, you're so perfect." Another slow, wet glide up into her.

"I loved watching you come. You're so beautiful when you come." She was biting her lip now and scrunching her brow, the picture of concentration.

"I could play with your pretty tits for days." He pinched her nipples again. This time, her moan was loud enough for him to hear. When she leaned into his hands, panting, he took it as encouragement to go a little harder.

His voice dropped lower. He was going to keep confessing. "I came all over you. When we made out in the storage room. It was so hot." She picked up her pace, and he matched it, jerkily, breaking their smooth rhythm.

Everything felt frantic and out of control. He was barely coherent. "I should come all over your tits right now. So pretty. Kneeling in front of me. That sassy mouth. God damn."

Everything hazed over. He was too far gone to stop. A roar filled his ears: above it, he heard her scream. Time stopped. He poured into her, clasping her tight as he let pleasure sweep him away. He was still babbling every thought he'd ever had about Simone, even as he jerked into her.

Awareness returned gradually. One hand was in her hair once again, while his other arm wrapped around her back, holding her snugly against his chest. His lungs were still working like he'd done a hard run, but the rest of him was loose and heavy. He could fall asleep like this, even sticky with sweat. Her weight on him was perfect. Comforting.

She raised herself to look at him, wincing when his hand stuck in her hair, like it always did. The edges of her hairline were damp.

How could she look so content and satisfied, yet so wary at the same time? What had he said to her? A vague memory returned to him: his declaration of love somewhere during the longest orgasm of his life. He wanted to push her away and start getting his equilibrium back. He wanted to hold her tight and stay inside her forever.

"Condom," she whispered. She rolled off to the side, letting him deal with it. He walked to the bathroom on still-wobbly legs, trying not to make a mess.

When he returned, she was in her robe, waiting to use the bathroom.

"I'm just going to rinse off."

"Okay." He moved out of her way, but at the last minute changed his mind, snagging her arm and turning her to face him. He leaned in, crowding her against the doorjamb. His dick tried to get excited at being naked and touching her again but failed. Too much activity for one day.

He put his mouth right at her ear, smiling when she automatically tilted her head to invite him closer. "Did you come, Simone?" Kissing down her jaw, he waited.

"Yes," she whispered.

"Good. If you hadn't, I'd join you in the shower and help you finish the job." He found her mouth and took it. The sheer joy of her lips on his would never get old. He poured all his longing and need into her, gratified when she twined her arms around his neck and desperately kissed him back. They stayed locked together for a long moment before he finally let her go.

The treadmill whirred mechanically under him, the pounding beat of his footsteps the only other sound. Sweat stung his eyes, soaking his shirt until it stuck to him, reminding him of last night's bathwater and slippery pleasures.

He'd guiltily tiptoed out when the gray-tinged light of dawn began to creep through the curtains. Restlessness had driven him away. That, and Simone sprawled naked and peaceful next to him. The sight of her had given him such a pang, he'd taken it as a sign to leave. He was gone before he found himself waking her with kisses or stroking her delightfully soft body. Before he wrapped his heart up with a bow and placed it reverently at her feet. God, he was so pathetic.

He had to think of something else. His dick was trying fruitlessly to come to life while all the blood in his body was otherwise occupied.

There was a shareholder meeting today over brunch. He'd have to have his wits about him for it, even though he would probably be expected to sit silently at Simone's side, as her *fiancé*. His stake in the company was only a few shares' worth—a gift from Frances at graduation that he had accepted with the best grace possible. He'd only ever been to one of these meetings and had avoided them ever since. Until he'd been finagled up here, he hadn't even known about the resort.

Putting his head in the sand was going to end, starting now. Even if he didn't get a chance to speak, at the very least he was committed to listening carefully to what this company was doing, both now and in the future.

He thought back through the weekend. Considering how Dick had treated him earlier, as her fiancé, James might actually be expected to start speaking for Simone. Of course, she had a larger percentage of ownership than he did, but Dick seemed to think women weren't interested in business. That he was right about Simone was coincidental. She was only around to keep her funding for the animal adoption center. He wondered what Dick thought about his own daughter's business smarts. Sam was intimately involved with the financials and projections, and Dick would be lost without her.

He ran on, barely noticing the slowly-accumulating miles, trying to sort out what he would say, or whether to speak at all. An image from the night before surfaced: of a determined woman standing in front of a much larger, more powerful man. If she could do all that she did, the least he could do was bring her work forward, at the very least making it harder to ignore.

When he got back to the room, dripping sweat but finally clear-headed, Simone was gone. Her message scrawled on the hotel notepad said she'd gone for coffee with Frances. He hoped she was giving her grandmother a piece of her mind, but knowing Simone, she was more likely smoothing things over.

It felt wrong to see her bags neatly packed and lined up by the door. He'd started to get used to seeing her things strewn on every available surface, but their stay here was coming to an end.

It struck him how much time they'd been indoors over the weekend. At one of the most beautiful spots in the area, surrounded by a sparkling lake and boreal forest, shield rock jutting out majestically between the trees, they'd spent hours on manicured grounds: beside chlorinated, temperature-controlled pools, in air-conditioned hotel rooms. A sterilized getaway, with nature playing a supporting role as an occasional scenic backdrop.

He shook his head. It was a shame, all of it.

FIFTEEN

Simone

The hotel restaurant was perfectly lovely, with great service and a flawless eggs benedict. Her coffee companion was the only thing bringing her down. Not for lack of effort on Gran's part, of course. Simone was just in no mood for all of Gran's usual patter. She picked up her cappuccino and let the flow of words wash over her meaninglessly, nodding in the right places, while her slowly simmering rage built and built.

"And I said to her, 'Joanne, there's nothing worse than lipstick on a pig. You and I both know that house has a crumbling foundation, and no amount of wallpaper is going to fix that. Look at the way the floor sags near the doorway.' She, of course, had nothing to say to that. She's never had my eye for detail."

Gran loved old homes and interior design. She and her friends would go to open houses and estate sales together just for something to do on a weekend.

If James had been at breakfast with her, the morning would be entirely different. She let herself daydream, just a little, picturing James seated across from her, digging into one of his typically huge breakfasts with delicate precision. She'd say something annoying just to get a reaction. Or maybe she'd flirt and watch him blush. If he was still capable of blushing after last night. She still couldn't believe she'd begged him to talk dirty to her. Of course, he'd done it in his own uniquely James-like way. Never quite what she expected. Alternately sweet, almost reverent, until her tears threatened to fall; and then filthy, making her so hot she'd nearly come on the spot. Whiplash.

He'd snuck out again this morning, though. No morning kisses, barely even a snuggle when she'd returned to bed the night before. She felt rebuffed. Well, she was the one who'd started all of this, and she'd deal with the consequences. Sauntering out with a condom in hand, as though she hadn't a care in the world: look where that had got her. Now, she was pining.

Consequences. It was time to dole them out, and not just accept them. She placed her cappuccino onto its saucer with a pointed click.

"So, Gran," she asked calmly, "Do you have anything to say about last night?"

Cut off mid-stream, Gran gaped like a fish for a microsecond, but she'd always been quick on her feet. "Simone, dear, you really must put that foolishness behind you. All a misunderstanding." She motioned to the server, trying to hurry the bill.

"I'd just like to know how much I'm worth, before I put it behind me. How many chips did I go for? What was the size of the pot?"

"Well, *really*. I can't be expected to remember that."

"So, you have nothing to say about it, then. No, 'sorry, Simone, for selling you to some gross man for a couple thousand dollars as though I own you?' Nothing at all?" It was the most sharply she'd ever spoken to her grandmother. Gran flinched.

"Well, darling, it was very unfortunate, that's all I'll say." The server came to her rescue, a little too promptly for Simone's taste. Gran signed the bill to her room with a flourish and an air of finality. From experience, Simone knew there would be nothing more.

"Now, darling, did I tell you that Joanne tried to outbid me on an exquisite turquoise necklace last weekend? I shot her down promptly, I don't mind saying that. Everyone knows turquoise is my color."

Simone was back to nodding dully. That had solved nothing.

She was still nursing her last few sips of her coffee when her cousin came into the restaurant, seating herself at the now-vacant place across from Simone. The staff brought her water and black coffee immediately, efficiently reappearing with a plate of toast almost before Simone could say good morning. Sam's preferences seemed well-known already.

Her cousin spread a thin layer of strawberry jam on one triangle of toast, then set it back in exactly the same spot as she sipped her coffee. "Simone, I'm not sure what's happening this weekend, but Mom told me about last night."

Simone waited for more, but Sam picked up her toast and started nibbling on one corner. Perhaps she was expected to fill in the blanks. She'd had just enough caffeine to start babbling. "I'm not sure what's happening either, and I'm not sure how you keep getting away with leaving early. All I know is I'm so mad at Gran that I could scream."

"I'd suggest saving the screams for the drive home. Mom told Dad about what happened at the table. From the sounds of it, he spent the entire night making Bob happy after you shut him down. I think they drank. Anyway, he's pissed, he's hungover, and I heard him talking about your funding in threatening tones."

Oh no. "Sam, they can't pull their charitable support, can they? It wouldn't look good for them."

Sam considered it for a moment and then winced sympathetically. "Frankly, I don't think it would be a problem. It was always Gran's pet project, if you'll excuse the pun. She does have a lot of sway as the majority shareholder, but she could be convinced to cast her vote another way." She tapped her lip thoughtfully. "They'd make a big announcement that they were donating to something very sympathetic, like cancer treatment. There would probably be a personal connection they could emphasize. No one would notice if they cut funding to the animal shelter."

"Not no one." She said it quietly, but Sam nodded in understanding. No one that mattered; that was the point. Simone sure as hell would notice if half her funding was cut. They already scrimped and saved wherever they could. "If they do cut it, how much time do I have to secure something else?"

Sam looked at her assessingly. "Smart, as always. The company committed for the year, of course. They won't back out of that because the budget was already approved.

Eleven months left in the fiscal year. You'd have time to apply for grants and funding."

Simone felt like crying. If she could patch things up with Uncle Dick, it would be far easier than dealing with a funding cut. Living with the uncertainty of scraping together grants and smaller charitable donations was so hard, she didn't know if she could do it. She swallowed back tears. "Thanks for telling me."

"Of course." She picked up her knife again, but paused. "It might be a net gain if it means cutting a few more strings. Something to consider." She eyed her, seeming to weigh whether to speak further. "For what it's worth, I like James. I always have. You seem happy together. I like how he listens to you."

Simone laughed. "Well, a compliant man may be the dream, but that's hardly James."

"No, I'm sorry, I wasn't clear. I meant he *hears* you. In this family, it's rare to be heard and seen for who you are, instead of what you can do for them." She smiled.

"I thought you were happy working for your dad." She'd never considered her cousin might be dissatisfied with her role. "I'm sorry. I shouldn't have assumed."

Sam waved her off with her knife, then dipped back into the jam. "I'm fine. I've just had a very prescribed life in many ways. There may be other things I could do with my talents, but leaving the family business would be seen as treason. I know they mean well. But it can be stifling."

"I understand. I hope that you find a path that feels more free." Simone checked the time and got up. She should collect James before it got too late.

"Simone, I'm going to have my assistant send you grant opportunities that I think you could qualify for. You should hear from us by the end of the week."

It was sweet of her, even if Simone wasn't ready for the kind of instability grant applications came along with. "Thank you."

She paused before she left the table. "We have a few very sweet kittens right now that would welcome a cuddle and a playdate, if you're interested." Sam had a few secret loves, kittens among them. Mabel had never allowed pets in the home, but Sam had helped Simone rescue more than one pregnant stray in their childhood. They'd kept them at Gran's house, of course, where Frances' granddaughters had been indulged in many ways they weren't at home. A memory of a much younger Sam, small and skinny, unhooking tiny claws from her jeans with infinite patience, surrounded by a whole litter of pouncing, rowdy kittens, flashed through her mind's eye. It was still one of her favorite childhood snapshots.

Sam smiled shyly. Maybe the same memories were playing through her mind, too. "I'll put it in my schedule."

SIXTEEN

James

The lobby was busy, but checking out only took moments. Then he was left with nothing to do but linger outside the meeting area and wait, desperately hoping that Simone would find him before anyone else did. Picking up pamphlets in the waiting area, he took a seat to study the touristy activities on offer—boats to rent, guided fishing trips, water skiing, and, of course, shopping in the nearby town of Tall Pines. Approaching footsteps interrupted his perusal of the town's highlights, and suddenly, a pair of feet wearing strappy heeled sandals had stopped right in front of him.

"Babycakes, you're alive." She laughed down at him, and the gray hues around him burst into riotous color. She was a sunrise.

He smiled back, casually, even while his heart clenched. She had another sundress on, all curves and flair and cleavage. This one was printed with red dachshunds on a dark blue background. Cute.

"Yeah, sorry. Wanted to get my run in before the drive." He tried not to look too guilty, keeping a casual smile plastered on.

"I figured when I saw your running shoes were gone." She didn't chide him about not leaving a note. He should have left a note. "Are you ready for one last session with my family?"

"How was your coffee? Did you hash it out?"

She sighed. "Not really. Gran said it was all a big misunderstanding and I should put it behind me. She seems determined that it's all over." Simone sighed again, gustily. "It didn't seem like she wanted to explain or apologize or anything. She brushed it off and talked about a necklace she bought."

"You didn't even talk about this whole charade we're doing?" He should have expected it, but he was surprised nonetheless. Frances still held a lot of sway over Simone.

She shrugged, defensively, he thought. "It's almost over, anyway. I didn't feel like getting into it with her." She continued, cutting off his protests. "We should go in."

He stood before she had a chance to step back, which brought them intimately close. He was so frustrated with her: with this weekend's aggravations, with her entire family, with the whole damn business. But he was still so drawn to her. Their thighs touched like magnets.

He let it all sit between them, and just looked at her, at her worried brown eyes, at her mouth pinched from stress. And it was enough—enough to drain away the tiny bit of his aggravation that was due to her, at least. He let his hands drop before he could take hers. It was impossible to know where they stood this morning. If only he hadn't left her to wake up alone, he might feel less unmoored.

"Let's go in, then," he said, reveling in the brush of his body against hers as he stepped past her. Her soft skin yielded wherever they touched, bringing the night before into vivid focus.

There was no way he should be able to keep moving apart from her. But he clenched his jaw and kept walking, impossibly, down the hall. Her steps echoed behind him, and he heard them with a guilty pang. He hadn't wanted Simone to think he was angry with her.

Shaking out his arms and stretching his neck, he stopped and waited for her, extending his hand. There was still a meeting to endure. Even though this whole thing was a farce, he would see it through. Even if she didn't think she needed backup with her family, he sure as hell did.

She slipped her fingers into his without comment, gracefully, in contrast to his tenseness. Her eyes searched his face: she nodded to herself without speaking. He was sure there was an entire conversation in her head he wasn't a part of, and couldn't bring himself to ask about. The engagement ring she still wore was prominent against his palm.

When they stepped into the meeting together, it was already full. The attendees were helping themselves to the generous buffet spread out on the side tables. He hadn't had breakfast yet, but the idea of eating here made him immediately lose his appetite.

Simone dropped his hand and started down the buffet table while he trailed beside her aimlessly. She shoved her full plate at him. "Go find a seat for us."

When she returned, she slid her first plate over to his spot and placed another beside it. He frowned, wondering why she hadn't eaten breakfast with Frances, but she was already flitting away.

He looked at their contents. Everything was something he would have picked for himself, right down to the flavor of Danish—cherry, naturally. She had even taken cantaloupe, her least favorite melon. The second plate held an omelet, another well-known dislike of hers. She'd gone through that buffet line twice for him?

Simone took her seat at last, setting down a tray with two cappuccinos and a small snack plate. After handing him one cup, she gestured at the spread in front of him. "Eat. I know you haven't had anything. Your brain is going to go all fuzzy if you're not careful. Plus, you're starting to get hangry on me."

He picked up his fork on autopilot and stabbed something at random. "I never get hangry. I'm always rational and dispassionate."

"Sure. Whatever you say, honeybuns." With a smirk, she lifted her cup and turned to greet the couple sitting across from them.

He ate steadily, his mood lifting as the plates cleared. Maybe it *had* been low blood sugar and a lack of caffeine getting him down. The buzz in the room didn't bother him anymore, not while he had Simone by his side, elegantly sipping at her coffee, making small talk with the people at their table so he could keep eating without interruption.

After everyone had been through the buffet line and found seats, Dick walked to the front of the meeting room and stood at the microphone. The speech he gave was more of what James had been hearing all weekend. Self-congratulatory, boasting to shareholders about how well this new venture was already performing and how bright its prospects were, lauding the partnerships being formed and the new opportunities in development. His brand manager followed, echoing the speech's contents, but with added buzzwords like 'synergy,' 'momentum,' and the ever-important 'paradigm shift.'

It was all meaningless, but James still followed it closely, searching for information amid the noise. The assembled members voted on a by-law change, then approved another director. All run-of-the-mill proceedings which no one seemed to take very seriously, judging by the way the brunch cocktails were flowing.

The time came for shareholders to discuss any other business. James stood as though pulled on a string, not missing Simone's quickly-concealed look of bewilderment. She really could pull an expression of polite interest out of nowhere when she needed to.

"James, my boy. Now that you're in the family, I knew you'd get more involved." Dick offered the microphone. "Come up here then, if you've got some business." He chuckled indulgently, in seeming disbelief that James could have anything serious to share.

"Thanks, *Dick*," he spoke into the microphone, emphasizing the name despite himself. "Yes, I'd like to discuss the permit process for the new resort, why it's in dispute, and whether the Anishinaabe of that unceded territory were consulted, and if so, what that consultation process looked like."

SEVENTEEN

Simone

Simone sat, stunned. The couple across the table looked over in shock. She smiled at them reassuringly, as though she had not a care in the world. Nothing to see here. This, at least, she could do. Holding it together, no matter what she might feel or think, was a specialty of hers.

The awkward silence that followed James's speech didn't last long, of course. Uncle Dick immediately re-took the microphone with the air of someone trying not to show they were sweating. He gave a clipped response about how all due procedures had been followed. But he couldn't seem to help himself at the end, adding that a few complainers hounded every project, and their real aim was to halt progress at every turn. It nearly turned into a rant, but Simone noticed the brand manager discreetly waving a quelling hand, and he abruptly cut himself off.

Bob leaped up for his turn at the microphone, yelling at James until the feedback screeched in their ears. It didn't take a genius to see where his diatribe was headed and didn't take long before he wound down to offensive slurs that made her hands tremble, curled into fists on her lap. There was nothing she could do about him. She was helpless in all of it.

Simone winced. This wasn't over: not by a long shot. Not for James, who was already standing to speak again, and certainly not for her. She could expect an email in her inbox by the time she got home, on the subjects of family members toeing the company line and keeping her fiancé under her control, with a few threats to withdraw funding from Helping Paws for good measure.

The plaster on her polite, interested smile was starting to crack around the edges, but she held on determinedly. It lasted through James' counterarguments: it turned out he had articles, *articles*, that he was referencing on his phone about the permit and consultation process. He quoted Dawn Bushie, apparently a well-known lawyer and journalist who had been gathering evidence of the consultation process's many deficiencies and publishing her findings in an independent newspaper. Amazing how he had all of this information readily at hand, but never once had she heard a word of it.

He must have been planning this from the minute she'd asked him to come. And again, not a word. The one person she could count on to always have her back had blindsided her, and she had no steady ground left.

He finally wound down, gesturing her way to include her—no, her *shares*—in his argument. "We formally request a full inquiry into the permit acquisition process and consultation process, including interviews with Indigenous leaders and area residents."

Simone stood in support, nodding as though she were completely along with him, even though what she wanted to do was rip off her ring and throw it at him in front of everyone. It would be a more meaningful gesture if he'd really given it to her in the first place.

They weren't a team, after all. Maybe they were just old friends who should have long ago gone their separate ways, who had been ignoring their vast differences. And the night before? Well, that had obviously been a mistake. Hurt weighed her down until she sank back unsteadily into her chair, desperately wishing this was all over.

James stalked back and sat down beside her, cheeks red with anger, a flush creeping down the back of his neck.

She leaned over and whispered, "I shouldn't have fed you. It's fueled you into insanity."

He didn't laugh. His mouth in a hard line, he was so serious, so determined. "This isn't a joke, Simone. Someone has to see justice done."

"What justice?" she hissed back, all patience gone. "I'm sure they have all the right permits and approvals. What are you expecting to gain from this?"

Uncle Dick was back at the microphone, wrestling it away from Bob, who had started yet another drunken tirade. She caught a glimpse of Aunt Mabel looking horrified and panicked, actually wringing her hands. She sympathized. She wouldn't mind doing some handwringing of her own. Gran was sipping her mimosa as cool as you please, with an occasional impatient gesture at Mabel to calm down. Nothing ruffled Gran for long. Sam was nowhere that she could see.

"It doesn't matter. If it's wrong, it's wrong, and they need to be stopped." His tone was so matter-of-fact it made her crazy.

"I can't believe you didn't talk to me about this. I can't believe you're messing everything up."

"And I can't believe you care so much about your precious status that you'll let injustice stand. Your family is being shady as hell, and you're here defending them."

They were both getting louder now, and the couple across from them were no longer bothering to hide that they were actively listening. The pair looked as though they were having the time of their lives. Like the conflict unfolding in front of them wasn't even real.

Fuck it. All of it. She could no longer be expected to please and appease everyone. A dramatic gesture was the only thing that would satisfy all the bubbling hurt and anger welling up in her. She pried the cursed engagement ring off her finger and smacked it down onto the table under her palm.

"We're done here." She got up and swept out of the room, not even pausing to see James's reaction.

Impulse and anger carried her all the way through to the lobby. Her bag was on the very top of a luggage cart, and she snagged it, barely slowing down. The ferry left at the top of every hour, and she had less than a minute to make it.

Running in a regular bra was never fun, but she clamped one arm over her breasts while juggling her purse and dragging her suitcase behind her. The boat operator saw her coming and waited while she charged down the dock, her suitcase bumping an angry staccato over the boards.

And then she was sitting in a big old paddle boat with nothing to do but feel those first inklings of guilt and regret that always followed rash behavior.

The wind drove the clouds across the sun, kicked the water into a choppy spray, and ripped her hair free to lash across her face. It mingled with the spray misting over her and the occasional tear that she couldn't quite hold back. She shivered and rummaged in her bag for a sweater. The slow boat bumped calmly over the swells, the captain seemingly unconcerned with wind, waves, and crying women.

It felt like it took no time at all to get across Bear Lake, so submerged was she in her self-pity. And then she was all alone on the dock, painfully aware that crossing the lake probably counted as her second impulsive act that morning. May as well make it a hat trick. She exited the dock and headed into town. Surely there was a coffee shop or a bookstore or something open on a Sunday. It wouldn't solve the problem of having left with no way to get home, but it would make her feel more in control.

Of all the stupid, impulsive shit she'd done, leaving the resort might well have been the worst. And worse yet—she was due to drive home with James. There was no way she could do it. Sitting beside him in a car for three hours after what had just happened? It was impossible.

The town had an adorable sign welcoming her to Tall Pines, which was quaint and seemed catered to tourists and seasonal cabin owners. Most of the shops were open, including a very cute cafe named Kindness Bean, staffed by a bored teenager reading a book at one of the tables.

She'd had too much coffee for one day, but she found a soothing-sounding herbal tea on the menu, then headed to the boardwalk, juggling her drink and her bags as she browsed through shop windows. Distracted, she ruminated over what to do next. She should call Gran and see if she could get picked up. She should text James and let him know he didn't have to drive her. She should call Uncle Dick and apologize profusely... that one stuck in her craw a bit. She had nothing to apologize for. None of it had been her fault.

One store seemed stuffed to the gills with kitschy knick knacks and signs painted with bears or deer. She wondered idly if she should get a hoodie printed with *Lake Life,* before moving on. The store on the other side of the cafe had a gorgeous display of high-end jewelry and handcrafts, which drew her past its door.

"Leave your suitcase outside. It won't go anywhere, and you'll never get it through my shop without knocking something over." The round-faced woman behind the counter was sitting with two kids—a baby she bounced and cooed to, and a school-aged boy with a serious expression who was working away in a notebook.

Simone backed out with an apology, leaving her bags in a neat array beside the door. She'd be able to see them through the glass. She hoped her purse wasn't large enough to cause comment. It might be safe to leave it out, but she was not at that level of small-town trust.

The aisles in the shop were narrow, but everything was meticulously laid out and displayed to its best advantage. Simone realized it was all Indigenous art: clothing, mukluks, moccasins, wall hangings, paintings and prints, and beadwork. The placards held information about each artist and their nation. She fingered some long, beaded earrings and glanced over at the cozy domestic scene behind the counter.

The shopkeeper was helping her kid spell a word, sounding out the letters, while skillfully keeping her baby's chubby fingers away from her two long black braids and the bright earrings dangling in front of them. Simone smiled to herself and picked out a striated set of beaded earrings. They'd be a perfect sunny accompaniment to one of her favorite sundresses.

"I'll take these," she said, laying them carefully on the counter out of the baby's reach.

"I'll have to tell Chantal how popular her work is. I can barely keep it stocked." She placed the baby in a bouncer suspended behind her, then gently nudged her kid's notebook out of the way so she could lay down paper to wrap the earrings. "You caught me just in time. I promised the kids we'd wait for their dad by the dock, so I'm closing up after this."

"Oh, does he work for the new resort?"

She snorted softly. "He's on a fishing trip. That place doesn't hire locals like him. And even when they do, my cousin found out they weren't offering much at all for guide work. He can earn more than triple on his own. It was robbery."

"Oh. That's a shame." Simone took a breath, tried to find the positive. "Well, your business will be booming this summer at least. All those new guests will probably help the area."

"Half my business is online, and I ship all over the world. We serve four nearby towns, plus we're a popular stop for people traveling through. We did just fine without the resort." She finished ringing up the sale.

"Um, do you by any chance know a Dawn Bushie? I hear she works with uh, Indigenous people? As a lawyer?" Ugh. That was so tentative she hated herself for it.

The woman snorted. "I mean, I don't know the woman personally. But yeah, she's well-known in the fight for land rights. Sometimes she even wins." She clucked her tongue and winked at her kid, who grinned back at her. "Too bad, now she's going to think all our people know each other."

"I'm sorry." Simone cringed.

She eyed Simone after printing her a receipt. "You come from the resort?"

She nodded. There didn't seem to be anything else to say.

"Well," she handed the bag over with an air of overlooking faults for the sake of politeness. "Next time, try the B&B on the edge of town. The food's better and the hosts are nicer." A bell chimed and she glanced over Simone's shoulder. "I bet that's your man now. He's got the look."

"Feel better?" The edge in that familiar voice behind her confirmed the other woman's instincts. It was indeed her man, kind of, and he was pissed.

She steeled herself before turning, but it didn't help. Waving goodbye to the shop owner, whose name she'd never asked for, she followed James out of the store.

It shouldn't be possible to be calmly furious, but somehow, he was pulling it off. His posture was relaxed, hands in his pockets, but the glint of feeble sunlight reflecting off his glasses couldn't hide the frustration in his eyes.

She opened her mouth, then shut it again, admitting to herself that she was pouting. Just the tiniest bit.

Somewhere beneath the pout, a quiet, insistent part of her whispered: that even mad, ashamed, and hurt, it was better to be with him than not. That part of her was glad he was here, even if they were about to fight. It was better than the alternative.

They stared at each other in silence.

Finally, he put his hand on her suitcase handle and jerked his head in the direction of the curb, where the car sat waiting. "Let's go home."

EIGHTEEN

James

"Here." She snagged his car sunglasses out of the console. He hadn't realized he was squinting.

The afternoon sun had finally broken fully through the clouds, just in time for them to head directly into its glare. The cool air from the vents fought a battle against the heat beating over the dash.

The drive should have been peaceful, but silence lay heavily between them. He was worn out by the turmoil of that morning, the worry of not being able to find her, and the mixture of relief and fury that had welled up when he finally had.

They wound through stately pines and frivolous quaking aspens, lit up into fluttering sparklers by the sun and the breeze. They were nature's glitter, the lighter side of each leaf flashing and turning in the sun. Gradually, his chest loosened, and his hands lay more lightly on the steering wheel, settling into the drive.

Over an hour passed before he glanced over at Simone, wondering if she'd fallen asleep. She was so quiet. But she too was staring out the window, face turned away from him and toward the colossal greenery flashing past.

He sighed. One of them would have to speak first. "Do you want to talk about it?"

Her voice still had a lot of snap for someone who'd been looking at trees for an hour. "About what, J? About having sex? About you hiding shit from me? About you trying to take down my family? Where do you want to start?"

"Yes," he retorted. "All of it."

"I just—I can't believe you would spring this on me. Not a word about it. *Nothing.* You could have told me anytime this weekend. On the drive up, or when we were in our room, when we were touring the grounds, or hell, even while you were inside me! *Anything* would have been better than what you did."

He winced. So fucking cavalier. She knew that he'd never had sex with anyone before her, and yet she just tossed off a remark like that. Like it was nothing. It hurt so much he couldn't breathe for a second. Maybe talking it out was a bad idea after all.

His voice came out even colder than he'd meant it to. "It's time for you to grow the fuck up, Simone. It's time for you to pay attention. Take responsibility. You can't keep hiding and claiming ignorance."

"My responsibility is to the animals, my volunteers, and my employees, James. I'm doing the best I can. I can't take on everything." She sounded defeated. He glanced over. A single tear tracked down one reddened cheek, though her voice hadn't even hitched.

He moderated his tone, pushing past his hurt to try to reason with her. "No one is asking you to. But your family is a powerful force. And what they do is all about greed and profit, stripping land and people of all their worth. You can't just wash your hands of it. Especially because you are profiting off of it. It makes you just as guilty."

She turned away again. He let it drop. Pushing her was never a good idea, but it felt as though they'd shifted a boundary that lay between them. The silence was less heavy. He indulged in a small fantasy of pulling over to the side of the road and gathering her in his arms, kissing her until she admitted that there was no one else she'd rather be with. If the shoulder on the highway was broader and the road a little less winding, he might have. And if he could have been sure he wouldn't be rejected. That wasn't something he'd be able to handle.

"I just don't know why you couldn't talk to me about it—why you had to spring it on me. I thought we were a team," she said finally.

"I should have. I know I should have. I chickened out."

"Why?" she asked flatly. "Why couldn't you tell me?"

"There was so much going on with Frances, with your family, with this farce we were supposed to put on. You know I don't do well with chaos. I was just trying to manage all my anxiety, to be there for you."

"Right, you sure were there for me in that meeting. Really had my back."

She wasn't getting it. "Simone, I'm on your side. I'm always on your side. You, caving to your family? That's not you. I'm trying to reach the Simone I know. The Simone I know would be furious at someone using her like your family used you. Frances basically sold you to that guy. Dick had you schmoozing. Mabel made you run all over the grounds taking promo pictures. They're all using you, and I don't understand why you're letting them."

"They're my family. I owe them. I need their support."

"Why? Is it just because of the shelter?"

She turned away again. He was getting tired of it.

"Gran." She said quietly. "She was everything to me growing up. The only one who understood me. Like, sure, she's impulsive, and a free spirit, and she drives my mom nuts, but then, so did I." She sighed. "I can't cut her out after everything she's done for me. After she funded the shelter, and with everything she's meant to me. In a lot of ways, she *is* me."

"She's not you, though. She's thoughtless. She cares more about her comfort than about her grandkid. She's all about instant gratification. You work hard, you care about other people, and if you do something on impulse that hurts someone else, you usually apologize." That *usually* hung in the air between them, but he couldn't take it back.

"You know how strict my mom was. Gran was like my pressure release valve. She still is. She let me drink wine, take in strays, wear makeup, and chat online for hours. She covered for me when I wanted to go hang out with you all evening."

"Simone, your parents might have been a little strict, but they were trying to protect you. Frances didn't give a shit about that. Not having boundaries isn't healthy, either." He knew this from experience.

"Regardless. I owe Gran and Uncle Dick for everything. For school tuition, for Helping Paws."

He needed to fight his mounting frustration before he could even respond. She was stubborn. As always. "You don't owe them for your tuition. You were a kid. Your education was not your responsibility. That's between your parents and them. You don't need to keep paying for it, keep all these damn strings."

She seemed doubtful, but at least she was listening. "But either way, I still owe them for the shelter. They didn't have to help me get it started."

"No, but they write it off for charity. It's not charity for you, it's for the animals. So again, they should be doing charity regardless; it's a write-off, and it doesn't go to you. You barely even take a salary, for fuck's sake. I do your income taxes. I know what you're trying to live off of."

"I make enough." She was beautiful when she was sulking. Even stolen glances were potent enough to make him dream again of stopping the car and kissing the petulance right off her lips.

The silence stretched even longer this time, long enough that the woods opened up and the road straightened out, big blue sky and open prairie extending as far as the eye could see. The sky met the horizon in a wide dome that made him feel like they were in a big fishbowl. Signs giving distances to the city came more frequently.

He sighed again, cracking the tension between them. They were always on each other's sides; he knew that much was true. Even if it didn't always feel like it. "I'm sorry for springing it on you. I'm not sorry for doing it, because I still think it had to be done. But I should have talked to you first."

When he looked over, she was staring right at him, cheek against the headrest. The highway's shoulder was wide here. Plenty of room to pull over and stare into her light brown eyes for a while, until they were okay again.

Instead, he turned his palm up in silent invitation and was rewarded when her hand slipped into his, her thumb brushing his skin in delicate, comforting circles. He hadn't realized how much he'd grown accustomed to her touch: what a relief it was to connect again. Her expression, caught in glances, was thoughtful, brow furrowed, facing straight ahead. No way of knowing what was going on in that active brain without asking. He decided to let her process.

Pulling up in front of her house and turning off the car, he could almost feel the toll of the weekend dragging at him like a physical weight. He got out to help her with her suitcase, then stood awkwardly beside her as she found the keys to her apartment. Her tears had long since dried, but she looked tired and crumpled and blotchy. Her lipstick was a faded stain, and her hair was a tangled knot on the top of her head. Even so, she was perfect. He didn't know what he was supposed to do, but he did know he wanted to lean in for a goodbye hug.

She turned away, keys in hand, and grabbed her suitcase handle. "I'll call you."

"Do you need help?" He pictured inviting himself in and settling onto the couch until he was comfortable enough that she wouldn't have the heart to kick him out, calm enough that she'd eventually start talking to him again. Maybe, in an ideal world, they'd even kiss. Angry kisses, because he was still frustrated with her.

Come to think of it, she always had been very frustrating. He could have been backing her against counters and walls and releasing their shared tensions for years. It was all one long missed opportunity.

There was no way her thoughts were headed in the same direction. She shook her head and gave him a halfhearted smile, already turning away. "I'll call you," she repeated lightly, as if she hadn't dashed all his hopes and made him hurt all over again.

NINETEEN

Simone

Snuffles whined and shook out his coat, spraying her head-to-toe with fat droplets. Droplets that smelled of wet dog. She always changed into her oldest stuff for dog washing, and that was saying something, because she never wore anything particularly new at the shelter anyway.

She spat, trying to get the wet fur taste out of her mouth.

"How's he doing?" Erica leaned over, staying well clear of the spray and damp. Her co-director had always been smart like that.

"Oh, he'll be okay. I wouldn't mind being a little less soaked, though." Erica was tall enough to capably corral a Great Dane in the bath, never mind a poodle-mix, but it was Simone's turn to get wet and dirty. She didn't really mind. She took her rotations, the same as everyone else.

The flea treatment was next, which brought about more whines. Snuffles didn't seem to like the smell. They were on a Sesame Street character name run—they always had a theme—but Snuffleupagus was a little too unwieldy for

regular speech, so his had been shortened almost immediately.

Getting the treatment through his thick, curly coat was
a bit of work, but she managed it. The dog had given up
whining and was standing there shivering, poor thing.

Erica had heard all about her disastrous weekend,
thanks to their early start together. Now she was hovering
as though she thought Simone shouldn't be left alone.

That was a recipe for getting roped into work. She
handed Erica a second towel. "There you go," she soothed
as they cocooned him. He rewarded each of them with a
happy pink tongue once they had him all wrapped up.

She laughed and snuggled him a little closer, even
though it was getting her very thoroughly damp.
He was sweet. Always offering kisses and thorough
tongue-bathings. Hopefully, the right home would come
up soon. She had a feeling about one of the applications
on her desk, that it would be the perfect fit for little
Snuffles.

Her days started early at the shelter, and she was always
prepared to come in for additional shifts any time there
was a sick animal, or to fill in scheduling gaps. It wasn't
easy, but it was her labor of love. Seeing the animals go to
good homes and caring for them while they waited was
all the reward she needed.

After making her rounds and chatting with the regular volunteers, she and Erica finally locked themselves in her office to hold the meeting that Simone had been anticipating all morning.

"I want to look into those grants we talked about last month and do a blitz on the applications that my cousin sent our way. We need more kennel space, and another staff member, and I want to operate as independently of Montgomery Developing as possible, in case their annual donation falls through next year."

Erica, her short black hair swinging, wrinkled her brow. "Have you heard something?"

"No, I just want to be prepared. I'm not in anyone's good graces right now, and I'm not sure if the shelter will feel the effects of that. We're all set for this year at least." Sam had sent another text reassuring her there was no way she could lose funding for this year.

Uncle Dick's emails had somehow managed to convey that he was apoplectic in only three lines, and her aunt had left two very shrill voice messages. Their good graces were the least of her concerns, however. She hadn't heard a thing from Gran, which in itself was something.

Erica snorted. "Frances had better have our backs. She'll lose her favorite dogsitter if she crosses me."

"Your vengeance will be swift and righteous."

"Damn straight."

They sorted through their grant application folder and picked out the most likely to start with.

"God, I hate writing about why we deserve money." Simone groaned.

"Well, I have mine picked out to start drafting. We can swap applications to keep our minds fresh. Catch each other's mistakes."

Simone sighed. "That will help." She reached over to clasp Erica's hand, then stared into her eyes solemnly, gearing up for her dramatic moment. "I want you to know that even though these things are my worst nightmare, and that red tape haunts my every waking moment, I will do *anything* to keep this going with you. Anything." She dramatically flung an arm to the heavens.

"Okay, geez, chill," Erica said, shaking her hand loose and laughing. "We'll figure it out. Just like we always have."

Simone nodded determinedly, and they got to work.

Later that day, she took a break from poring over her applications to work on their social media and fundraising plan. They had a good following, but they could always do more to stay on the radar of potential donors, and to keep on top of the algorithms that showed their posts to followers.

Eyes blurring, hours later, she finally packed up. It was miraculous that everything had been quiet. Her office usually had a revolving door, so Erica must have magically kept people away. Simone put it on her list to bring treats for the volunteers and an extra something for Erica's kids.

She was almost done her grocery shopping before she realized she hadn't thought of what she would make for James. It was possible he wasn't expecting anything from her after their uneasy parting, but she didn't intend to renege on her side of their disastrous bargain. She traced her way back through the store to add chicken to her cart.

Finally back at home, snacking on veggies and dip and fresh pita bread from the bakery, she threw together a lemony chicken and rice casserole. The recipe was simple enough to let her mind wander while she hummed along to her favorite cooking playlist. Once the casserole was in the oven, she started on cookies for the volunteers. The freezer was still stocked with homemade dog treats; she took out some to thaw. Everyone would get cookies tomorrow.

She kept checking her phone as she worked. It sat silently, mocking her. There was one person she needed to talk to. And it would have to be her who reached out. She picked it up and swiped through to her call screen.

"Hi Gran. Do you have time to talk?"

"Oh, darling. How are you? I was so worried about you." Gran sounded breezy as usual, but it struck Simone as false.

"So worried, but you didn't call?"

"Oh well, you know there was just so much silliness happening. And you and James were both so upset, I thought you needed time to deal with each other. I know you must be very angry with him, darling. It was terrible of him to make such a scene. Mabel was in total shock. I thought she might faint, poor dear."

Ah. So, she was supposed to offer up James as the sacrificial lamb on the altar of her family's embarrassment. Side with them against him. Disavow him and ideally never bring him around again. Well, Gran didn't know her as well as she thought, if that was the case.

"I'm actually not angry with him. We had a long talk on the drive home. The person I'm angry with is you." She said it neutrally, but she knew it would be like dropping a bomb. Of course, she and James still had things to work through. But her anger had been directed to the wrong place. The real betrayal was from Gran.

"I'm not sure why you would be upset with me, dear. It was all James."

Simone found herself pinching the bridge of her nose and shook her head. Now she was borrowing his coping mechanisms. "I guess you've already forgotten everything with Bob Taggert? It was like nothing to you, to what? Promise that I'd date that horrible man? Sleep with him, maybe?"

"There you go, blowing everything out of proportion again. It was just a little joke. It wasn't anything serious."

"Gran, it was serious enough that you got me to bring James as my shield from this man, and then, surprise, we're engaged on top of all that? What about that is not serious to you?"

She sputtered, but Simone cut her off.

"Next time you have some problem or scrape that you've gotten yourself into, for the love of everything holy, leave me out of it. If you cared about me at all, you wouldn't have asked me to be anywhere near that horrible man. And you wouldn't have asked me to play along with your lie, or involved James." She stopped, surprised that she was close to tears.

It had taken the smallest amount of time for the engagement lie to begin feeling all too true. It now seemed absurd that they hadn't been together forever, that they never cuddled, that he'd always been so protective of his personal space. The new James, the one who touched her, who nuzzled her temple, who held her hand constantly—he'd felt like the James she should have known all along. She'd met a new Simone too. One that begged for what she needed, who confessed feelings, who'd let him in. Which was the true version of them?

Gran had nothing more to say to her, other than a feeble, "Of course I care, darling." Simone hung up with a curt goodbye.

There was nothing to do but keep going down the family list. She pulled out her laptop and finally responded to Uncle Dick, after a long time spent composing, deleting, recomposing, and rewording. She copied in Aunt Mabel. There was no way Simone was going to call her back.

In between trays of cookies, she started some more research. She'd need the right people to talk to. It might take a while to set things in motion, but she was determined to do better this time. Even if her scheme wasn't perfect, at least she was now paying attention.

It was late before she finally closed her computer and packed away all the cooled cookies. She still didn't know where she stood with James, but as for the rest, she was ready to start.

TWENTY

James

The photographer's link in his email looked so innocuous, the accompanying message casual and chirpy. Lana obviously hadn't heard what had happened at the shareholder meeting. He clicked on it nonchalantly, opening a shared album that derailed his day completely.

He couldn't believe how they looked at each other in these images. Her face dreamily stared up at him, his expression as though he would offer the moon to make her his. Everything he'd felt was laid out so starkly, the emotions in each perfectly lit, composed, and touched-up photo leaping from the screen. They looked at each other like they couldn't bear to be apart. And yet here they were, separate.

He missed her so much.

There were so many to go through, he gave up on the file he'd been working on. There they were on the golf course. Here they were kissing. Here beside the pool, sharing a sidelong look that held so much promise. Here they were at the lake, silhouetted against the setting sun, totally absorbed in each other, seemingly moments away from stripping down right there and devouring each other.

It was all here in front of him: photographic evidence that what had happened that weekend was not a delusion or a fantasy. It had started to feel dreamlike: long, slow days in bright sunlight filtering through trees, stolen touches, secretive smiles, and so much heat.

Most of all, he remembered her scent surrounding him, lime and mint, and so fresh. Her lips curving right before they met his. Her body moving over him. Graceful, beautiful, soft, and generous. Textures came to him as he stared at the photos: her bouncy hair, dimpled flesh, the fascinating striations of her stretch marks. He feared the impressions would fade, that he couldn't possibly remember the full glory of her. Every morning he woke and wished it were still real.

But more than wishing he could touch her, he missed being claimed by her. He'd been proud to be with her, to bask in her glow. To show his delight in her openly, to protect her, and have her leap to protect him. However briefly, they had almost been a unit. Them against the world.

They had both lost their way somehow. She was still so desperate for her family's approval. And there was no denying he had mucked it up. If they really were friends, he should have been able to tell her. When she had asked him why he hadn't, he'd surprised himself with his answer.

His third time through the photo album, now safely stored on his computer, he finally admitted he wasn't getting anything else done that day. Undocking his laptop, he packed some files to work on at home.

His house was so orderly upon entering, so soothing, that his shoulders loosened immediately. It reminded him of his mom. Going from chaos to order always did. Before even realizing it, he had his phone in his hand to call her.

"Jamie. You okay?" Her voice still had that distinctive rasp, though she'd quit smoking ages ago. It was always the first thing she asked him. She did care, deeply. Even if she couldn't always take care of him in the way he might have wanted.

"Yeah, mom. Everything's fine. I'm just calling to see if your grocery delivery was right this week, or if I need to get you anything."

"Oh, well. They gave me the wrong creamer again. I never liked that hazelnut stuff."

"I'll go pick up your usual tomorrow before work and drop it off, okay? And maybe after, we can go through that box of magazines you wanted to look at?"

"Well, I'm not so sure." She sounded guarded, protective, as always, of her stuff. She had a problem with things accumulating. He could vaguely remember a time when the house had been clean, before his dad's job loss, the drinking, the yelling, the divorce. Now he tried to clear out enough that the house was at least sanitary and not hazardous to her health, but boxes of paper and bins of clothes were still piled in every room and on every surface. It was almost impossible to convince her to part with anything.

"Drina says there's a sale at the thrift store where you can fill a bag for a dollar. Can you imagine?" she asked eagerly.

"That's fun, Mom. Maybe we can take a bag or two to the thrift store to donate and go together?" He didn't know how to help her, so he tried to enable her in the least harmful way possible. "Oh, I paid your cable bill and the electric, and your spending money is in your account now." He didn't know how to help her, but he could keep her finances straight, and had for a long time. Giving your mom an allowance as a teenager was a crash course in budgeting that most people didn't get.

They spoke a little longer about her friend Drina, about whether she had anything she could donate, and which toys she was setting aside for her grandchildren. These were the same topics as usual, and they gave him just as much of a pang as they always did.

Reassured that she was fine, he hung up and settled at his dining table with his computer again. Before he opened his client files, he had to peek into that photo album one more time. Would it be creepy to order some prints, just for him?

Not that it was weird to have pictures of her. He had one on the wall opposite—in her grad dress, his date for the night, even though she'd been dating some guy from her school named Tom at the time. She'd always been popular there.

His high school friends had always liked her when she came around to hang out. They'd all had fun that night: she'd slipped in seamlessly with his friend group, teasing the guys, chatting with everyone, drawing out anyone hanging back. But she'd come for him, getting prettied up for a second graduation party. She'd reworn her grad dress, got her hair done again, made a big deal of being his date, and even danced with him, just as friends. They both looked happy in that picture, but he was the one who looked like he couldn't believe his luck.

She was his longest and most stable friendship. She knew a bit about his home life; she'd hid with him in his treehouse when things were bad. None of his other friends had ever come to his house or known anything about his family.

Why didn't you tell me? There was an entire mountain of things left unsaid between them. Even when he'd asked her to grad, it had been as a friend, so casually she couldn't possibly have known his palms were sweating as he did it. He'd never once made a move, never even considered it after she confessed, with many blushes in junior high, that she'd kissed someone at her friend's birthday party. Spin the Bottle had never before crushed someone's heart and hopes so completely. From that moment on, it was clear to him that Simone was interested in other people, and could never be interested in him.

Never once had he rocked the boat on their friendship. How could he? How could he risk messing up the closest relationship of his life with unwanted feelings?

It was just that now, after the past weekend, all of that seemed ridiculous. Maybe this had been between them the whole time. What if she had been his date for real at grad, and they had ended that night with stolen kisses in the back of the party bus? What if he could have been sharing all the feelings he usually kept clamped down tight? What if they could have done this all hand in hand, all along?

A knock at the door interrupted his spiral. He opened it, and there she was, like he had conjured her just by thinking about all their possible pasts and missed opportunities.

He blinked down at her, standing there with her hands full of bags and parcels. Her dark brown waves were pulled up into a knot at the top of her head, and she was sweating, her sunglasses slipping down her nose. She had obviously come straight from Helping Paws because she was wearing jeans and a ribbed tank instead of one of her sundresses. He was still in his work clothes and hadn't even loosened his tie. He felt ridiculously overdressed.

"Are you going to let me in?" she asked, half laughing, half exasperated.

"Right." He stepped back. "What's all this stuff?" He took bags as they were thrust at him and plopped them on the table.

"Your meals. I'm a little late, but I never go back on a bargain." She smiled, and he got tangled in it, hardly remembering what they were talking about. She fanned her face, then actually lifted the edge of her tank to wipe the sweat from her hairline, showing off an expanse of soft stomach and one of her neon sports bras.

"Meals," he repeated obtusely. Reaching around the bags, he closed the laptop, where a picture of them mid-embrace was prominently displayed. Then he headed to the kitchen to get her some ice water. She must be too warm.

"Uh, yeah. You—" she cleared her throat awkward-ly—"agreed to do that weekend with me, and I agreed to make you meals. And pie. I made that, too. God, it's too hot to make pastry. The butter got so soft I could barely get the crust in the pan. Plus, there are cookies, because I was baking them anyway for the volunteers."

"You made me pie." He smiled and moved toward her. She took a step back that seemed automatic, so he stopped and held out the glass as a peace offering. She didn't want him in her space.

"Oh hey, did you get the pictures from Lana?"

"Yeah, I saw them." Saw, obsessed over, no need to go into specifics.

"I emailed her back. We never signed a waiver, so they can't use them for resort promo purposes. I said I was sorry to waste her time, but she didn't care. She's being paid regardless. She sent her congratulations again. I think she's hoping we'll consider her for the wedding."

All he could manage was a grunt in reply. What was he supposed to say to that? Wordlessly, he held out the glass again.

She laughed as she took it, an anxious titter that put his teeth on edge. Why was she nervous around him? He hated that they were being this awkward. It made his despair from earlier rise like a fog, obscuring even her beautiful face.

"I can't stay, but I wanted to give you that. And there's a special shareholder meeting being called that I'd like you to come to if you can. Next week Wednesday."

"I doubt your family wants me there, Simone."

"I don't care. I want you there." The fog lifted, letting him see the fierce determination in her eyes, giving him hope. "I need you there. If you can come."

"For you? Of course."

TWENTY-ONE
Simone

All eyes were on her. She stepped closer to the microphone and winced at the way it picked up her anxious breathing. Trying to calm herself, she looked around the room again. All the usual suspects were there, except James. Her heart sank that he hadn't been able to make it. Well, she wasn't doing this for him. Except for the parts of her that *were* doing it for him. She was a jumble of conflicting thoughts and feelings.

She caught Gran's eye. Their phone call earlier in the week had been new territory.

I'd like you to do this for me, please, Gran.

Well, I'm not sure that I should.

Gran, what good is all that voting power if you only ever use it to give the board unnecessary trips to the Bahamas for meetings?

All right. If it's important to you, I'll back you. Dick won't be happy.

Is he ever? May as well give him something worthwhile to complain about.

She smoothed her skirt over her hips with one hand and plucked the mic out of the stand with the other. With or without him, she was doing this.

"I am informing the shareholders of my decision to transfer my shares in Montgomery Developing to Dawn Bushie. She represents the surrounding community for the next Northern Tides resort and will bring her valuable perspective to all future Montgomery projects. Ms. Bushie has said she looks forward to examining the plans in detail. Frances Larson has approved the transfer."

To her right, she heard Uncle Dick reacting. But she had eyes only for the tall, slim figure who had recently arrived and stood at the back of the room. He had come. "I am also following up on a question posed at the previous stakeholder meeting. I have heard from more than one national journalist who is very interested in Montgomery Developing's permit application process. I request that a formal inquiry be launched and that the results be made public."

The room was silent. She went on, speaking directly to her aunt and uncle now. "I have always thought I would be proud of my family's legacy. I am grateful for the education I received, and for the way you support the animal shelter.

But I will not stand by and let this family do harm for my profit."

That was the end of her prepared speech, and she hadn't even come up with anything to wrap it up. Gran had agreed to push the request through, following Dawn's guidance on how to structure the inquiry. It might be the beginning of the end for the company, depending on the results, but Gran had agreed anyway, and Simone would hold her to it.

Thanking them for their time seemed farcical. Instead, she set the mic back in its stand and walked away, to low murmurs. She walked to the back of the room, where she held out her hand, and James took it. They walked out together.

It was surprising to be out in the sunshine after the artificial lights of the conference room. The statement she'd made had been short and to the point, but it had drained so much out of her that it felt as though hours had passed.

She turned to James, pulling him to a stop with a tug on his hand. "So, I don't know if you want to transfer your shares, too. I kept one. Just so that I could still be officially nosy if I needed to. You could keep one too, if you wanted. But if you add yours to mine, that means a bigger profit share for Dawn, and I have no doubt she'll use it for something good. Hell, even if she uses it to pamper herself, it'll be for the best. From the conversation I had with her, sounds like she could use a vacation."

She was babbling now, but he stood patiently looking down at her, listening intently.

"Dawn was great, really. She remembered me from that weekend, and we had a long talk about the best course of action. I wasn't sure if she'd want to sit on that board, but it didn't seem to faze her. She said she was looking forward to doing some disruption. Plus, she said after getting through law school, it would be a picnic."

There was nothing left for her to tell him, and he still wasn't talking. "Are you going to say anything?"

"What made you change your mind?" he asked softly.

"I thought about what you said. That I didn't have to keep trying to please my aunt and uncle. And Gran. I talked to her too. She had nothing to say that made any sense. I think you're right that she doesn't show her love in the way I need or hoped." She cleared her throat. "I want to be more like you are. To do the right thing, even when it's hard. You've always been so brave, and you always take care of everyone. And I've been so selfish and cowardly. There are so many things I've been avoiding dealing with for too long."

"No. I am so proud of you. I'm always proud of you." He took her hand in his, and she realized she had been trembling. He gathered her up into a slow, soothing embrace. She sighed and hugged him back.

"I just don't see how you could be," she mumbled into his chest. He squeezed her tighter for a moment, then loosened his arms.

She pulled back to look him in the face again. Apologizing had never been her strength, but she was getting practice today. "I'm sorry. I shouldn't have dragged you out there and carried through with that weird fake engagement thing. And I definitely shouldn't have abandoned you after the shareholder meeting and run off. I still can't believe I did that."

"One of your more impulsive moments. It's okay. I've already forgiven you." His arms dropped and he moved away from her. It was too bad the hugging was over. She'd liked that part.

"I still wish you had told me. I need to hear the truth from you, even when you're worried, and even when it's hard. I need to know what's going on. Even if it's not something we can fix, at least we can share whatever problem it is."

"I know. I'm sorry too. I'll try to share more." He grabbed her hand again, tugging her in the direction of the parking lot.

"That's it, then? We're all good, water under the bridge, nothing else to talk about?" She was fishing, which she generally had a firm policy against, but really, the man was being impossible, towing her toward the cars.

"Maybe a few more things to talk about. Come on, I want to take you somewhere. I'll bring you back to your car later."

She let him hustle her into his vehicle. They took winding streets and back ways, avoiding traffic, on streets bracketed by spreading elms that made a shadowed canopy beneath the evening sunshine. James seemed to have no conversation to offer, and the small talk she tried to start was met with such halfhearted one-word answers that she eventually gave up. His mom was fine. His job was good; his gamer friends were doing well. She stared out the window, at a loss for words.

He didn't seem to want to talk about anything else that had happened that weekend. And if he wasn't going to bring it up, she wasn't going to humiliate herself.

Had his first time been so traumatizing that he was never going to acknowledge it again? He'd certainly seemed enthusiastic in the moment. It had felt like their minds were intertwined, as though she could see straight into the heart of him, as though they'd been connected and in perfect harmony. But now, she wondered how that was even possible. It must have been an illusion of the moment, easily shattered. Very easily, since he'd left first thing the next morning and never looked back.

And yet she could sense a new openness between them. They were finally seeing each other at last. Their weekend together had shaken them out of old routines and taken them to a new depth. And even if it hurt, she would not lose this new level to their friendship. He was too important to her. Even if they never spoke of that weekend again, their emotional intimacy would remain, if she had anything to do with it.

She'd just have to get over the rest. The dating apps were waiting for her, whether she wanted them or not. Maybe if she sifted through enough dross, she'd find someone worth having a conversation with.

"Where are we going?" she asked abruptly. She knew this area well. "Is your mom okay?"

He looked over at her sideways. "I told you, she's fine. We're just revisiting an old favorite."

An old favorite what? Movie? Game? *Wait.* "If you think these arms are strong enough to get me up a rope ladder these days, you better think again."

He just grinned at her.

TWENTY-TWO

James

"You'd better not be looking up my skirt." Her voice drifted from above him, tremulous.

The rope ladder had been cut down many years back, but it had been so long since she'd been in the treehouse, she would have had no way of knowing that. He'd brought out the sturdy straight ladder he used each spring to make repairs, propping its edge against the trapdoor opening, and was firmly holding it at the base for her to climb. It was solidly planted and wouldn't have shifted even if he hadn't been holding it, but he wanted her to feel safe.

"You're wearing shorts underneath. There's not much to see." They happened to be delightfully snug and semi-sheer—bright pink today—and watching her from this angle was an absolute pleasure regardless of what she was wearing, but he looked away dutifully. He could use a bit more blood to his brain anyway, if he was going to get through this.

"Oh, you've made it beautiful!" Her voice was delighted, though muffled by its location from halfway inside the treehouse.

Her delight was a balm. It partially soothed the nerves churning in his stomach.

"Are you coming?" He looked up. She was already inside, peering down to see what he was doing.

"Sorry. Be right there." He raced along the ladder, laughing when she scolded him about not being careful enough. "This thing is low enough that I can jump down from here. I'll be fine." He pushed the ladder out of the way, letting it fall to the ground with a metallic clang, then closed the trapdoor.

She rolled her eyes. "I hope those handholds are as sturdy as you seem to think they are." He still had slats bolted into the side of the tree that he used whenever he was climbing up alone, rather than repairing things or carting stuff up.

"It'll be fine." He locked the trapdoor by sliding shut the wooden latch perpendicular to the opening. It was pure habit. No one was chasing him anymore.

She was already sitting cross-legged on a cushion that he'd laid out beside the little rug in the middle of the floor, appearing right at home. Nerves threatened to overwhelm him again, but he moved over to the insulated bag he'd hauled up earlier, spread a few clean kitchen towels on the floor between them, then started unloading the picnic he'd packed.

"What's all this?" That delight again. Surprising her was one of the best things on the planet.

"You've missed dinner. I thought we could come up here, to eat and talk and watch the sunset. Just like old times." He finished laying everything out, then uncorked a small bottle of champagne. The clerk had told him it was good. The champagne flute he handed her was plastic, but she didn't seem to care, taking it with a grin and toasting it against his glass of sparkling water. They filled their plates with nuts, fruit, cheese, cured meat, and crusty bread spread with tapenade.

Simone certainly seemed happy, nibbling at the spread and sipping her champagne while admiring the view out the window, noticing the changes he'd made to make the interior more comfortable. She exclaimed over the low storage bench he'd added beside one of the windows. The wonder she brought to everything, the joy she took in the smallest details, made his heart clench painfully in his chest. She was the light in his life. She always had been.

She was too damn good for him, but he didn't care.

He cleared his throat. "Do you remember the last time we were here?"

"Must have been ages ago. I don't think we ever came up during the last few years of high school. I'd assumed it had rotted out or something. You always came over to my place or Gran's, or we went to hang out with your friends, remember?" She was still dreamily staring out the window. "I can't believe you've kept it so nice all these years. I missed this place." She looked at him then, more sharply. "Why didn't we come here more often? Just because of your dad?" Her expression turned tentative.

"I usually wanted to be somewhere else because of him, yeah." He cleared his throat again. "It feels ridiculous to admit this, but that's not the reason we never came back here."

"Why then? What's ridiculous?" She was half smiling, anticipating a joke.

"The last time you were here, you told me you'd kissed someone at a party. I, uh, had a pretty big crush on you. And that day, my hope died that maybe you'd want to kiss me or date me. I started trying to get a little more distance. So, I stopped inviting you over as much and tried to just be your friend, because that's all you wanted." He tried to take a casual pull at his drink, but, just as they had the last time he'd swigged sparkling water, the bubbles tickled his throat and made him cough. He was making a mess of things.

He looked over at her, trying to figure out what she was thinking. There was red in her cheeks. A lot of red. She hadn't said a word, but she looked guilty.

"What is it?" he asked, suspicious.

Fidgeting with the cheese on her plate, she avoided his eyes. Her flush crept down her throat. It was fascinating to watch her turn three shades of crimson in front of him. Fascinating and confusing. What did she have to be embarrassed about? He was the one who'd been an idiot. He was the one trying to work up the courage to bare his soul to her now.

"Is it hot in here?" She fanned herself.

"Not particularly. Answer the question."

She sighed. "So, the reason that I told you I'd kissed someone, not that it wasn't true, but maybe a little exaggerated..." Her glass wavered in her hand, and she trailed off.

"How exactly was it exaggerated?" He couldn't believe it—she was unraveling right in front of him.

"Well, it wasn't much of a kiss, really. I chickened out of the full spin-the-bottle experience and just gave that guy a peck on the cheek. What was his name? Steve?"

"That's not how you made it sound," he said slowly. "Why did you make it seem like you'd made out in a closet for an hour?"

She gave a mortified groan. "I was trying to make you jealous," she whispered into her plastic champagne flute. "You didn't seem to care, so I, um, decided to move on. I started dating the first person who paid any attention to me." She grimaced. "That guy was a mistake. Live and learn."

There was nothing to do but stare at her, blinking in disbelief, while he tried to process the last however many years of his life in light of this completely new information. "Jealous?"

"It was my big dumb plan to get you to kiss me, maybe, or at least act in a way that I'd know you wanted to."

"Simone, you know me better than anyone in the whole world. What on earth made you think that would work?"

"In hindsight, it was idiotic. I should have just grabbed you and kissed you instead." She smirked, her redness starting to recede, her equanimity regained now that her confession had been made. "Or maybe I should've just pretended that my grandma needed us to date."

"Wait. Don't tell me you made that up, too?"

"No. I promise, that weekend was not me. I just can't help but wonder if we would've been able to have this talk earlier." She wiped her hands on one of the cloth napkins. "Ever since that disastrous day in our friendship, I've had a policy against fishing for information. And maybe against trying to make someone jealous enough to grab me and kiss me. Because that backfired bigtime." She smiled. "So, I'll ask you straight. Do you want to make out?"

He couldn't help but laugh, even though adrenaline was still making him feel sick to his stomach. "I want so much more than that, Simone. I want what we have together and everything we could have together. I want our history and our future. I want you. It feels like I've been holding myself back from falling in love with you my whole life. And that ridiculous weekend shoved me right over the cliff." He made himself meet her eyes. She was wiping away tears. She was so beautiful.

There was too much shit in the way. He gathered up everything carefully, folding the corners of the towels, and unceremoniously dumped it all into the soft-sided cooler, not bothering to put the leftovers away properly. It would have to keep. She placed their glasses to the side, while he moved her nearly-full split of champagne.

With deliberate care, he crawled toward her in that low space. He was holding himself together until he could hold her. She welcomed him with a mischievous smile, blinking back the tears that still lingered in her eyes.

"Kiss me then, and I'll follow you over the edge," she murmured.

It was all the invitation he needed.

TWENTY-THREE
Simone

Each kiss they shared was brand new, every moment a revelation. This time, their hunger was below the surface, simmering, and tenderness was foremost. It felt like love, like infinite care. The setting sun washed them in pink and gold, suspending them in time, catching them in amber light.

Falling in love was such a misnomer. She was soaring.

After many long moments, they wound back to earth together. His smile was so delighted that she almost couldn't look directly at him, at his face lit in coral hues, the sunset glinting off his glasses.

"Let's keep doing that. Often. Like all the time." His smile split wider, but his tone was very earnest.

"It's a deal."

He nodded, taking the hand she'd offered to shake on it, holding it in his and rubbing his thumb over her knuckles. It was a nontraditional way to seal a deal, but she didn't mind.

Still holding her hand, he reached back into the basket with his other arm, rummaging through awkwardly. She laughed and tried to pull away so he could look properly, but he tutted and held her firm. Finally, he came up with a familiar velvet ring box, holding it so she could see it.

"I called Frances and let her know I still had it. She told me it was yours to keep, that it suits you." He tried to give it back to her, to fold it into the hand he still held.

She stopped him and closed his fingers around it. "I'd like you to keep it for me. Until I ask for it back." She tried to communicate what she meant, without actually saying it straight out. You didn't bring up engagement after a few kisses and one night together, did you? Or were the rules different if you'd already been fake-engaged? Was it different if you'd known each other for a lifetime?

He nodded solemnly, adorably, the tiniest flush on the tops of his cheekbones making her want to smile wickedly. She'd like to see him very flustered again—as soon as possible, if she had her way.

"I understand. I'll keep it. Until you want me to give it to you again."

His eyes, looking into hers, were so full of love and understanding that she almost stuck out her left hand and asked for it right then and there. She may not have been on the best terms with Gran, but she loved that ring. From the first moment he'd put it on her finger, she'd wished its meaning was real.

"Oh no. What are we going to tell your mom?" The mortifying realization that they were in his mother's backyard suddenly hit her. Tammy had probably seen them climbing up and was wondering what they were doing.

"She already knows what we came here for. Actually, we'll probably have to go in for a bit. She'll have coffee on and want to chat if that's okay?"

"Of course. I'd love to catch up with Tammy."

"The house is a little cluttered. I haven't had time to help her get organized. And the coffee will be instant."

"I understand," she said gently. "I'd never judge your mom. You know that."

"I know." He clenched and unclenched his hands as though he was working up to leaving, then smiled distractedly, gathering the few last things still left out and reorganizing everything he'd dumped in earlier.

"Why don't you let me do that and go fetch the ladder for me instead?"

He nodded. Opening the trap door, he dangled his feet through the opening, then pushed off into a heart-stopping, loose-limbed drop. Some things never changed.

By the time he popped his head back through the hatch to take the basket from her, she had everything packed.

The trip down the ladder seemed so much shorter than the journey up.

Tammy gave the biggest grin when she saw them come in hand in hand and hugged them both in turn. She was in her usual jeans and a plain tee, but she'd put a little lipstick on and her faded blond curls were patted into a neat round shape. Simone had always liked Tammy, who'd been kind enough to listen to all of Simone's incessant chatter as a kid.

"Well, he finally got off his butt and gathered the courage to talk to you, did he?"

"Mom," James said warningly.

"What? It's a mom's job to be embarrassing. Especially watching you pine after your girl for so long. I'm allowed to rib you about it, just a little."

"I'm going to go fix the coffee." James stalked off with his shoulders around his ears. His mom watched him go, fondly.

"He always was a sensitive one, my kid. And I liked how you looked after each other. Your parents are going to be thrilled, too. I tried calling your ma, but I got her voicemail."

"Oh, yeah, they're still away, and she's never very good at checking her messages when she's with my aunt. Not back till the end of the month." She groaned inwardly. She was going to need an epically long visit with her parents to catch them up when they got back.

By the time James returned with the coffee, Tammy and Simone were going through old photo albums, carefully peeling apart old plastic pages to revisit her and James's growing-up years together. Old friends whose names she'd forgotten, favorite swimming spots, and summertimes full of skinned knees and sticky popsicles all paraded past as she flipped through. There they were in formalwear, dressed up for his graduation celebrations. She'd had the most fun that night, a better time than her own grad with her actual boyfriend. There she was at his university grad, wearing his mortarboard, clutching his gown-clad arm playfully and cheesing for the camera. He was smiling at her instead.

It was almost too much. Too much history, too much time being seen and known so deeply, both as she was then and as she had grown to be. All of it folded into who they were now, but that was so much less than what she hoped they could build together. Simone blinked away tears for what felt like the fifth time that night, tuning back into the conversation to hear James gently arguing with his mom about whether she should be keeping his old National Geographic magazines.

"Why don't James and I go through them together? We can take them with us when we go tonight. Then you won't have to think about them anymore."

"You take that album too. I want Jamie to copy those photos for you. You can print the ones you want to keep."

They left laden with boxes and bags of pictures, but Simone felt light. James also looked buoyant as he loaded the cargo into his trunk.

"So." He turned to her when they were both settled in the car. The look he gave her somehow managed to be simultaneously shy and almost sly. "I know you have to be at work early, but I love getting up early. Driving you back to your car in the morning sounds like the perfect way to wake up." He checked his watch. "We have plenty of time to stop by your place for some clothes if you want to stay over."

"Why, James Randall, what a shocking proposition." She took his chin in her hand. "I accept."

Epilogue

Simone informed him this was called a "foster fail." But it was all over for him the moment he'd decided to call the little abandoned kitten Catan. Get it? Because he was a cat. Who had...settled in their home. It was fate.

Simone also claimed that there had to be some Siamese in the cat, because no regular cat yowled like that. But James liked that they could have a full conversation anytime he needed someone to bounce ideas off of.

"I still don't think that cat is actually participating in your brainstorming session."

"You're just jealous because he likes me more." Catan perched on his shoulder, his favorite spot in the house. He liked heights. Simone said, snarkily, that it was so he could look down on everyone. But Catan couldn't help his natural superiority.

"We are *never* fostering again. With your soft heart? It's hopeless." She paused to consider, the employee scheduling sheets arrayed on the table in front of her momentarily forgotten. "Maybe a turtle? No, you'd somehow find a way to develop an affection for a reptile."

He shrugged, nearly dislodging Catan, who dug in his claws. "Sorry, buddy." He patted Cat's head in apology. "The problem is naming them. If you brought home a turtle, I'd have to name it Shell Shock. Then I'd have to keep it forever. You can't just let Shell Shock go, after that."

"I guess I should be glad house rules apply to me, too. You're not getting rid of me, Babycakes." She looked down at the ring on her finger and grinned.

Catan, though he yowled in protest, had to give up his shoulder perch. Because James suddenly had a very pretty girl to kiss.

Thanks so much for reading! I'm thrilled my labor of love is finally out in the world.

If you enjoyed it, please consider helping other readers find it by leaving a review. Thank you!

I'd love to keep in touch, and you can sign up for my newsletter to read an exclusive bonus snippet! You've seen the fake engagement; now it's finally time for the real thing. Download your bonus here!

Acknowledgments

I wrote this book as a settler on Treaty 1 territory. It is the territory of the Anishinaabeg, Nehethowuk (Cree), Anishininew (Oji-Cree), Dakota Oyate, and Denesuline (Dene) Peoples, and the homeland of the Métis Nation.

Big thank you to Lisa, for the sensitivity read. Any mistakes with regard to Indigenous representation, or the depiction of the ongoing fight for land rights, are my own.

This book would not be here without the support of, and harassment by, a few very special alpha readers. It takes a unique kind of love and care to read those messy first drafts as they come. Your boost was enough to make me feel like I could keep going—bit by bit, and mess by mess. Alexis, Blair, Becci, and Kim: thank you for putting me in writer jail and continually demanding chapters.

Many thanks to my editor, Bittersweet Reads, for all the comments, encouragement, quibbles, healthy skepticism, and painstaking attention to detail. You made this book better. We and our time-blind, ADHD selves finally pulled it together, and I couldn't be more proud of what we accomplished.

Shout out to the group chat for your unwavering and unhinged support. Love you.

Many thanks to the HB NaNo writing group for the sprints and commiseration.

Thanks to beta readers, Meredith, Holly, Marty, Lauren, and Lucy. Your insight made the book stronger.

Thanks to the extremely multi-talented Brynn for my cover art. Working with you is a dream, and your gifts are astounding.

Finally, thanks to my partner, who is my forever cheer-leader and believes in me even when I've nearly given up. I love you.

About the Author

Lynn Camden is a settler in Treaty 1 territory on the beautiful Canadian prairies. She's always looking for romance that thrills and for the coziest possible reading nooks. She began writing her debut novel to combat pandemic doldrums and swiftly fell in love with writing. When she's not writing, Lynn can be found baking with her kids, watching bad action movies with her husband, sipping margaritas, or gossiping with friends. Connect at www.lynncamden.com.

Also By

Set in Stone: an Elmdale Romance

www.ingramcontent.com/pod-product-compliance
Lightning Source LLC
Chambersburg PA
CBHW072008210726
48294CB00013B/1727